# Curve Ball

John Danakas

James Lorimer & Company, Publishers
Toronto, 1993

James Lorimer & Company Ltd. acknowledges with thanks the support of the Canada Council, the Ontario Arts Council and the Ontario Publishing Centre in the development of writing and publishing in Canada.

Cover illustration: Daniel Shelton

**Canadian Cataloguing in Publication Data**

Danakas, John
    Curve ball

ISBN 1-55028-423-1 (bound)
ISBN 1-55028-433-9 (pbk.)

I. Title.

PS8557.A63C8 1993   jC813'.54 C(93-094450-X
PZ7.D36Cu 1993

James Lorimer & Company Ltd., Publishers
35 Britain Street
Toronto, Ontario M5A 1R7

Printed and bound in Canada

Many thanks for suggesting ways to improve the manuscript to my editor at James Lorimer & Company, Diane Young, my friend Peter McPhee, and my wife Sophia; and for their continual support, to my parents Gus and Mary Danakas.

# Contents

# 1

# A Bad Dream

I'm in an airplane, far above the clouds, breaking in my brand new catcher's mitt. I smack the pocket of the stiff new mitt with my right fist. That softens the leather and makes the mitt open and close easier.

It's also a good way of letting out my anger.

You see, the reason I'm up in this plane squished between an old man with thick-lens glasses and a businesswoman pecking at a laptop computer is my mom decided to send me to my uncle's for the summer holidays.

I'm pretty mad about that. I mean, I had my own plans. The baseball team I play on, the Jarvis Badgers, enters the City of Toronto Little League playoffs next week. Last year our squad made it to the semi-finals, and this year we expect to go all the way in the eleven-year-old division. We have a solid team of all-around players and a real genuine pitching ace in Danny Frankenheimer.

But now I won't be there to celebrate with the guys at the victory party. No, I'll be in Winnipeg, Manitoba, helping out at my uncle's hamburger joint.

And I say rats to that.

Mom couldn't care less. She's working all summer and doesn't want me hanging around the house alone all day. We live downtown in a neighbourhood that isn't considered too great a place for kids.

"Mom, can't I just stay home like last summer? At least until the end of baseball season," I pleaded after school a few weeks ago. I thought I was being reasonable. But just try reasoning with adults.

"No, Tom," my mom had answered back in her *It's final!* tone of voice. "I'm not letting you stay in the city all summer. It's not good for you. If I could be home with you, it would be different. I'm sorry about your baseball team and I'm sorry about your buddies, but you're not staying in Toronto this summer."

Then Mom worked out a deal for me. I had my choice between some corny summer camp up north or one month at my Uncle Nick's place. He lives alone behind his diner out in Winnipeg and apparently is just dying to spend the summer with me. Mom says Uncle Nick's place is almost like living out in the country. Uncle Nick's my mom's younger brother. I've never met him before and I'm not too keen on flipping burgers for him all summer long. But then again, I've always hated summer camp.

The deciding factor between my two awful choices ended up being Uncle Nick's promise that I could play with the local Little League baseball team if I spent the summer with him. Since I wouldn't be able to play organized ball at summer camp, that sealed it. And then Mom sweetened the pot by buying me this really expensive Ernie Whitt model catcher's mitt that I could use in Manitoba. Ernie Whitt used to be the batcatcher for the Toronto Blue Jays. He's my favourite player. I even have a baseball signed by him outside the Jays' old ballpark, Exhibition Stadium. Uncle Nick's place it was going to be.

So here I am sitting in a DC-9 headed for Winnipeg, pounding away at my new mitt. The best way to work in a new glove is to stuff a hardball in the pocket and tie some rope tightly around the whole glove, then wedge it underneath a bookcase or something heavy like that for a few days. But I don't have that kind of time. Mom bought the mitt just two days ago, and I want it ready for my first practice in Winnipeg.

The best I can do is smack the mitt good and hard, beating it quickly into shape. The leather smells rich and strong and feels soft and smooth around my hand. I keep bringing the mitt up to my nose and smelling it like I do when I crack open a new comic book. I like that brand new smell.

At the same time, I'm hoping with all the hope I can muster that the kids my age up in Winnipeg have a decent baseball club. Their regular season's probably ending this month just like ours, so there's no use joining them if they're not going to make it to the playoffs. I don't expect to play much anyhow because the team must already have a starting batcatcher, but I'll take anything I can.

Anything.

A few innings behind the plate. A few swipes at bat.

Because I love baseball.

Most kids I know want to be the next Wayne Gretzky or Mario Lemieux. But I'm not into hockey. I'd much rather be the next Ernie Whitt or Johnny Bench. I play batcatcher. Have since I first signed up for organized ball when I was just a seven-year-old pipsqueak with a bad arm and weak knees. I can meet the ball often enough with my bat to keep my average over .300, but it's behind the plate where I do my best work.

When you're the catcher, you're the hub of the whole team. Heck, if you play right field, you might as well pick daisies for most of the game. Or daydream about playing catcher. But when you're behind the plate, you can count on being in the thick of the action on every play. I like it that way. After I play ball, I go home with my uniform mussed up and dirty like those clothes you see on laundry detergent commercials. Mom's not too happy about that, but I am. It usually means I've had a great game.

A flight attendant comes by now with a tray of airplane food. I pass on it and just stare outside at the dark clouds rolling under the plane's wing like smoke out of a volcano. I'm hoping Winnipeg will be fun, but I'm afraid it will be a boring town where the kids don't give a hoot about any sport but hockey. I mean, they don't even have a baseball team in the major leagues.

And what about Uncle Nick? What's he going to be like? I can't say I expect too much. For one thing, Mom's warned me that he can't speak English too well. Only Greek. Mom tries to speak Greek to me every once in a while and forces me to go to Greek School twice a week in an old church off Danforth Avenue, so I understand more than a few words, but I'm not sure I know enough of the language to communicate with a guy all day long.

That's another problem. This whole idea of spending the summer at Uncle Nick's is full of problems. And the biggest problem is my mom doesn't realize that.

But it's too late now. I fold my mitt tightly shut and shove it under my rear end. That should help break in the pocket. Then I leaf through the magazine in the seat pouch in front of me. But it's full of goofy ads and the word search has been figured out by the passenger before me. I snoop into what the businesswoman is typing out on her computer. Doesn't look interesting. As for the old man on the other side of me, his nose is poked into a thick paperback. He hasn't lifted his head since we took off, except once, to listen to the flight attendant explain what we're all supposed to do in case of a crash landing. Must be a good book. It's certainly a long one.

I nod off then. I dream Uncle Nick actually turns out to be Ernie Whitt and over the summer he teaches me everything he knows about playing batcatcher. It's a great dream, the kind that's so much fun you want to keep on sleeping and dreaming forever.

About an hour later, I wake up to the co-pilot's voice over the intercom telling us we'll be landing in Winnipeg soon. The temperature there is twenty degrees celsius, he says. That's warm. Baseball warm. I cross my fingers and hope for the best.

The plane's engines all of a sudden rev up and flaps slide out like escalator steps from underneath the wings. I look outside the window and see we're slicing through clouds, white now not black. One second we're covered in puffy clouds and I can't see anything, and the next second there's a flash of blue sky.

Then the plane starts bucking. I'm not scared because I've been on a plane once before and this is nothing unusual, but the old man next to me is holding on for dear life. I feel like maybe telling him there's nothing to worry about, then figure, why not just let him suffer. I'm in that kind of mood.

Meanwhile, the businesswoman's fingers are flying over her keyboard like she's in her own private office. Nothing disturbs her. I lean over her to peer out the window and she doesn't seem to mind.

I'm searching the ground down there for some baseball diamonds, which in my book would be a sign of intelligent life. But all I can make out are a bunch of swimming pools and the odd soccer field. This doesn't look good.

The houses look Monopoly-sized from up here. They're neatly arranged around two zigzagging rivers. Where the rivers meet there's a cluster of highrise buildings you could fit into one block of downtown Toronto. This Winnipeg's small-time, if you ask me.

In no time the plane's wheels touch down with a sharp screech and we're coasting down the runway to the gate. I get excited and undo my seatbelt, drawing a dirty look from the old man beside me. Nuts to him.

I tuck my mitt into my armpit and wait for the plane to make a full stop. Just as it does, I hop into the aisle and slip past a few folks to get farther up in the line. Sometimes it pays to be a kid.

I have no idea what Uncle Nick looks like. Mom described him for me before I left, but I didn't listen to a word she said. At the time, I was trying to block out this whole ugly experience.

But there's no blocking anything out now. I'm off the plane, scooting past passengers, almost running through the gate, wondering what in the world I'm doing in this strange city. The flight attendant who's supposed to hand me over to my uncle can't keep up. I feel the same way I did the time I got lost when I missed my subway stop. Everything's a blur, kind of unreal, and you're just waiting for it all to end. I feel like Mom's pulled this awful practical joke on me. I'm almost sure I'm not going to like my Uncle Nick.

As I race down the steps in the airport terminal, I scan the crowd for someone who might be my Uncle Nick. I spot him right away. You couldn't miss him. He's short and bald. A round belly bulges out of his green windbreaker and a thick black moustache sprouts from underneath his nose. He looks just like those men who play cards and backgammon all day in the Greek coffeehouses on the Danforth strip. He's the man in the crowd who looks the least like Ernie Whitt, so I know he must be my uncle.

Sure enough, this guy reaches out to hug me and plants a kiss on each of my cheeks, the way my mom sometimes will ever since Dad died. Uncle Nick's all smiles and he gazes at me, saying over and over, "What a big boy! What a big boy!" like he's never seen an eleven-year-old kid up close before.

I'm embarrassed and shrug myself away. I figure the whole airport's staring at us.

Uncle Nick takes hold of my hand, squeezing hard, and says, "Tommy, we are going to have a wonderful time this summer."

Somehow I don't believe him. And I hate being called *Tommy*! Besides, I'm not sure I even want to have a good time here. I already miss my teammates on the Badgers. They're going to go all the way this year. Without me.

Just then Uncle Nick puts his arm around my shoulders and leads me to the luggage belt. He keeps looking at me and smiling. I may be down, but he's happy.

I wish I could run away right now, but there's nowhere to go. I hate this. I may be in the middle of a crowded airport in a strange city thousands of kilometres away from home, being hugged by an uncle I don't even know and I'm not sure I like, but I'm silently praying this is all a bad dream, and I'll wake up any minute now, crouched behind the plate at Jarvis Park, waiting for Danny Frankenheimer's next pitch.

Trouble is, I don't wake up. And this isn't all a bad dream.

# 2

## Uncle Nick's Diner

All the way to Uncle Nick's diner I'm scoping out the window for baseball diamonds. I don't notice any. As I peer over the long front end of Uncle Nick's Riviera, I wonder when to ask him about his promise to Mom to let me play Little League ball. I figure the time isn't right yet.

I'm still nervous. It's uncomfortable sitting inside a car next to someone you don't even know. I keep squeezing my new catcher's mitt. That makes me feel better. When I'm not looking out for baseball diamonds, I'm sneaking peeks at Uncle Nick, trying to make out what kind of guy he is. On the plane I decided to be mean to him and everybody else here, in order to punish them since I'd much rather be home. But he's making it difficult for me.

Whenever he talks to me, it's like he already knows me. He doesn't say much, but he asks a few questions about Mom. How she's doing, what her job at the sewing factory's like.

The next thing I know, Uncle Nick's doing a great imitation of Mom when she's mad. He gets down perfectly the way her face scrunches up like she's just blown out the candles on a birthday cake. I can't help laughing.

As for his English, it's a lot better than Mom led me to expect. He's got an accent, but it doesn't seem to hold him down. It's no trouble talking with him.

I also have to admit I like the way he drives. I classify adults by the way they drive. Mom is a turtle, so slow I just sit back and sleep and tell her to wake me up when we get there. She avoids the 401 at all costs. My cousin Ari, he's a real hothead, a lucky one at that, just missing an accident by a millimetre or two every other block. But Uncle Nick's a cool driver. He knows what he's doing. He works his gear shift like a real pro, and we glide in and out of lanes smoothly.

Mom was right about Winnipeg. It *is* a lot like the country. I notice a lot of trees and grass. Everything is flat and spread out. But so what. I want baseball diamonds, not picnic grounds.

I can't wait to get to Uncle Nick's place and just relax. It's been a long day. Uncle Nick notices I'm restless and tells me we're almost home.

I roll down my window to get some fresh air. Right away I wish I hadn't. A heavy, strong smell attacks my nose. It's kind of a farm smell.

"*Pheww!*" I say. "What's that?"

Uncle Nick laughs. "You'll get used to it," he says. "That smell comes from all these big buildings you see around us. They're meat-packing plants. They make all sorts of things like steaks and salami and wieners here and ship them out to supermarkets and restaurants. Most of my customers work at those plants."

I can make out the buildings and smokestacks rising up alongside them. I take a good look because I've never seen a meat-packing plant before. But the smell is awful.

In a second we make a quick turn and Uncle Nick taps me on the shoulder excitedly. "This is the diner right here," he says, parking the car with a sudden stop and pointing to the building in front of us. "I hope you like it." The street sign at the end of the parking lot reads Frontenac Street.

Uncle Nick's restaurant is certainly a neat-looking place. It's called the Olympic Diner. You can tell that right away because high above the front door a neon sign flashes OLYMPIC DINER in gold letters. What's neat is that between the two words, between the C and the D, there's a little orange torch that flickers on and off, as if it is bursting into flames. It's really something. I look at the sign for a few seconds before we walk in, just watching the way it works, the tiny flame licking outward, the gold letters glowing in the dark so that you can see their reflection on the cement of the parking lot out front.

Uncle Nick notices me admiring the sign and chuckles. "That was my idea, you know," he says, proudly. "I had that sign put up right after I bought the place, almost twelve years ago, about when you were born."

We go in then. Uncle Nick lets me walk ahead of him, his right hand behind my back. Inside, the diner looks real old, like something you'd see in a black-and-white movie. A battered pinball machine with some flashy space ship art is sandwiched into the far corner. A wooden lunch counter runs across the length of the diner, with a half-dozen red-topped revolving stools set up in front. Colourful cardboard cutouts of different foods and drinks — a hamburger, an ice cream cone, a milkshake — decorate the walls. A chalkboard with "Dinner Special" scrawled on it rests against the cash register. Behind the counter is the kitchen. To get there, you push through a swing door. There's a barbecue, a pressure cooker, a huge fryer filled with oil, a milkshake machine, and a bunch of other things whose use I can't figure out.

A woman steps out from behind the counter, wiping her hands on her long apron. Her hair is dark black and pushed up high over her head. There's a bright red band of lipstick across her mouth. She looks a lot older than my mom, but she looks neat and clean, like she's trying her best to make herself and this place look young.

"Vera, come over here," Uncle Nick calls out to her. "I want you to meet my nephew Tommy."

Vera walks to me with her right hand stretched out to meet mine. "I've known Nick here for a long time, but have never met a relative of his," she says. "I was beginning to think he didn't have any, that he was a loner just like me."

I say, "Pleased to meet you," and actually mean it. Underneath that lipstick, Vera has a soft, easy smile that I really like.

"He looks a lot like you, Nick. The brown eyes. Around the forehead. Only he's got a little more hair." She tousles my hair and laughs. I begin to worry that maybe I look as Greek as Uncle Nick.

Uncle Nick has taken off his windbreaker and is slipping on an apron. It has sauce stains on it. Vera steps behind him, grabbing the loose strings of the apron and tying them into a knot for Uncle Nick. These two are a real team.

I sit down on one of the red-topped stools. Silver studs rim the red leather. I run my fingers over the studs.

"Hear you're a real baseball star, Tommy," Vera says, swinging an imaginary baseball bat. "Your Uncle Nick tells me you two are visiting the community club tonight to get you signed up on a team."

That's a relief. I don't think I would have been able to sleep tonight unless I knew for sure that I'd be playing baseball here this summer. Vera knew what I wanted to hear. I like that.

Uncle Nick shows me to my room. His house is attached to the diner through a door at the back of the kitchen. There's a damp smell to the place, kind of like a basement, and mustard-coloured carpeting that looks old and worn covers the floor. I can tell right away that Uncle Nick cares more about the restaurant than his house back here. I guess all he does here is sleep. My bed is in a little area just off the living room, separated from it by a thick brown curtain. There's a single bed and a night table with a lamp. That's about it. I don't say anything but make a face like, *This isn't exactly the Holiday Inn.* I can tell Uncle Nick's hurt. I decide I'd better say something. Something nice.

"I like it here. It'll be OK."

That's mostly a lie, but it does the trick. Uncle Nick is smiling again. I guess because Uncle Nick's a bachelor, the place isn't in the neatest condition. But I don't mind. Less of a chance of messing anything up, like I always end up doing at home.

"Tommy, I'm going back to the diner now. We should be getting some customers from the meat-packing plants. The late shift is having their dinner break. As soon as the dinner hour's over we'll walk over to the community club to sign you up on the baseball team. Rest for an hour or so and then come out and I'll have something special for you to eat."

Uncle Nick's trying hard to be nice to me. So's Vera. I don't know what to make of all this. To be honest, I think I wanted to hate it here.

When I'm alone I lie back on the bed and look up at the ceiling. Two cracks meet at one corner forming what look like the jagged pieces of a puzzle. I stare at them, my mind wandering. Right now I have no idea what's coming next for me. And I can't stand that. The suspense eats at my stomach.

I lift myself off the bed. I take my mitt and put it underneath my pillow. Then I take my suitcase and flop it on the bed. I start putting away my things in the drawer of the night table and in a closet at the end of the room.

Uncle Nick has piles of old racing car magazines in there, and I flip through a few. After a while I decide it's time I went back to the diner. Even though I'm used to being alone all the time, because I don't have any brothers or sisters, all of a sudden I'm lonely. Deep-down lonely. A strange place'll do that to you.

The Olympic Diner is empty, except for two customers hunched over coffees at the counter. I take a seat on one of the stools. Uncle Nick is at the barbecue cooking hamburgers. He's got four hamburger patties on there now. Steam rises from the burgers in thin ribbons. Flames from the barbecue lick the underside of the patties, making a sizzling sound. You can almost taste the burgers just by sniffing the air.

Uncle Nick flips the patties when they're cooked on one side and I can see the muscles of his wrists stand out like strands of rope. When the patties are completely cooked, he slides them into buns and places them carefully on white plates, all in one swift motion. One of those plates, heaped with french fries, he passes over to me.

I take a bite from the burger Uncle Nick has made for me. It's great. It's meaty and spicy, just like the hamburgers Mom makes when we have a barbecue. Just then the phone rings.

"Good evening, Olympic Diner. What can I do for you?" Uncle Nick answers eagerly. "Who's this? Super Burger? . . .

But . . . Well . . ." Uncle Nick's face droops like a scoop of ice cream melting.

"Vinegar? OK, I'll bring it down myself. You don't have to send anyone." Uncle Nick wipes some sweat from his forehead with the back of his hand. "Yes, two cases. I won't forget."

Uncle Nick hangs up. Then he shakes his head and sighs."Super Burger wants to buy two cases of vinegar from me."

"The nerve of those bullies!" Vera exclaims.

"They're my neighbours, I have to help them out," Uncle Nick says, trying to explain. "Tommy, grab two cases of vinegar bottles from the shelf in the back. We're going to take them across the street to Super Burger. They've been so busy they've run out. It's on our way to the community club anyhow."

There are two Super Burgers in my neighbourhood in Toronto and there must be at least one in every city on the planet. The one across the street from the Olympic Diner looks the same as the others except it's brand-spanking new.

I carry one case of vinegar, Uncle Nick the other. The case isn't too heavy, and I curl it up and down from my legs to my shoulders to work on my biceps. When you're a ballplayer, it's good to get as much exercise as you can.

Super Burger is as crowded as the Eaton Centre a week before Christmas. People and cars are everywhere. Uncle Nick and I have to dodge customers just to make our way to the front counter.

GRAND OPENING balloons hang from the ceiling. The workers behind the counter all wear bright blue uniforms. The menu is up on a long, bright sheet of plastic above the counter. Kids are playing in a section of the restaurant made to look like a pirate ship. Shiny orange plastic seats are arranged in neat rows throughout the whole restaurant.

There's a smell in here, but it's not that rich, restaurant smell of the Olympic Diner. It's more plasticky, like the inside of a new car. You can't taste anything in this air.

The manager recognizes Uncle Nick and rushes out to greet him. He's pretty young. His hair is slicked back and he's wearing wire-rim glasses. I don't like him. Uncle Nick is trying to be polite, but he looks kind of dazed to me. He keeps looking around at the place, nodding his head slowly.

Meanwhile, the Super Burger manager is being super nice — too nice. He pays for the vinegar and offers Uncle Nick a cup of coffee.

Uncle Nick says no to the coffee, explaining that he's kind of in a hurry. The manager nods his head and says, "Come back soon. We should talk. We can help one another out."

How? I wonder. I don't get it. Why was the manager so nice to Uncle Nick? He acted like he was up to something. And why did Uncle Nick look so sad in there?

As soon as we step outside, Uncle Nick takes a deep breath of the night air, like he's just had to run through an obstacle course. Then he turns to me, and I can make out a smile breaking across his face.

"Well, Tommy, I guess it's time to sign you up on a baseball team so this summer won't be all work for you."

That's exactly what I want to hear. I flash on a vision of me in a batter's stance at home plate in a Little League game.

"I can't wait to take a few swings in a real game," I say to Uncle Nick. "Just to feel the bat smack the ball."

A puzzled expression passes over Uncle Nick's face, and he scratches his ear. He looks like I've just shoved a Rubik's Cube into his hands.

"Tommy, I wish I knew something about baseball," he begins. "You're going to be playing on the team this summer and I'll come watch as many of your games as I can, but I won't understand a thing that's going on. Not a thing. I've been in Canada now for almost twenty years and I know all about football and hockey. But baseball!? I've tried to watch baseball on TV a hundred times and I still don't know what they're doing."

"It's easy, it really is."

"Two people play the game and the rest just seem to be watching. It doesn't make sense."

I have to laugh. I've never heard anyone describe baseball that way before.

Then Uncle Nick digs into his jacket pocket. He pulls out something I've never seen before. It's obviously a dried fruit, but I don't know what kind. The skin is leathery and golden brown. It looks almost like a miniature battered old baseball mitt.

"Ever tried a dried fig?" Uncle Nick asks me, popping the fruit into his mouth like it's a jelly bean.

"A dried fig?!" I say. "*Yechh*!"

"Don't be so quick with that," he says. "Your mother and I were raised on these. On our farm in Greece we have dozens of fig trees. The figs grow round and green in August and then we leave them out to dry in the sun. Try one."

I take one in my hands. It's squooshy like a bean bag or something.

"C'mon, try it," Uncle Nick says, as he pops another into his mouth. "It's a good energy food. If you eat one during a baseball game you'll never get tired."

I close my eyes and take a bite of the fig. It's really sweet and chewy. The inside tastes almost like jam. I actually like it. A lot.

"Not bad," I say, licking my lips.

"So you liked it? Here's some more. Save them for your games."

He hands me about a half-dozen dried figs. I squeeze them into my pockets, thinking the guys'll think I'm crazy if I have one of these during a game instead of a candy bar.

"Thanks," I say.

In a few minutes we're at the community club. Three baseball diamonds, a soccer field and a wading pool surround the clubhouse, which looks like a white wood shack. WINDSOR PARK RED SOX is painted in fat green letters across the front of the clubhouse.

Uncle Nick leads me inside. At the far end a woman is sitting at a desk. She looks like someone's mother. A clipboard with pages sticking out of it lies in front of her.

"They told me I could still sign my nephew up for baseball," Uncle Nick says.

"What age?" the woman asks.

"Eleven," I answer. I don't know why, but I feel butterflies in my stomach.

The woman breathes in and out slowly. "I'm sorry. The eleven-year-old team is full. Too many kids signed up this year and the coach just couldn't find a spot for them all. The club in Norwood is a little far but they need players, and some of our boys have signed up for their team."

Those butterflies in my stomach start spinning around down there. I don't have a bike and I know Uncle Nick won't have the time to drive me across town for practices and games.

"Are you sure there's no room?" I ask. Sometimes people make mistakes.

"Yes," the woman replies quickly. "In fact, all our baseball teams are packed except the twelve year olds'. One of their boys has already left for the summer and they're looking for a player."

Uncle Nick pipes in right then. "Tommy, how about trying to play with the twelve year olds?" He looks at me seriously. Something in his eyes tells me he thinks I can do it.

"I don't know," I say. I want to play baseball, but with kids my age. I'm not sure I'd be good enough to play with twelve year olds.

"You can do it," Uncle Nick says.

"I suppose I can try out for them," I say. That's how bad I want to play baseball.

The woman looks up at Uncle Nick. "You'll have to sign this form that says you'll let Tommy play for the team, and I'll make sure it's OK with the coach."

"Of course I'll sign," Uncle Nick says.

I'm worried about playing with twelve year olds, but I'm more excited about playing baseball, period. And if this team needs players, at least I probably won't have to ride the bench. My stomach settles down. I'm going to play ball after all.

"The next practice is on Diamond A tomorrow afternoon at four. Report to Coach Minuk, and he'll take it from there. Good luck."

Tomorrow afternoon! I can't believe it. But it's not too soon for me. I want to play baseball. Right now wouldn't be too soon for my first practice.

Playing with twelve year olds might be hard. I wonder if I'll be good enough. I wonder if one of those players who left on their holidays was a catcher. I wonder if I'll be the smallest guy in the lineup. And I wonder how fast these twelve year olds can throw. Back in Toronto, I know a twelve-year-old pitcher, Frankie Mastella, who has even mastered a deadly curve ball.

Will I be able to hit off these guys? More importantly, will I be able to catch their pitches?

# 3

# New on the Team

I like getting to practices early. That way you warm up slow and easy. But for my first practice here in Winnipeg, being new and all, I decide I don't want to be the first guy out on the diamond. The other guys might think I'm weird, a keener. So I grab my catcher's mitt only about five minutes before practice time and tramp over to the community club, so nervous my knees wobble and my legs noodle like spaghetti.

I fantasize about what it would be like to just once in my life walk out onto a diamond and have everybody figure right away that I'm a great player. I know I'm a pretty good ballplayer, but I'm always having to prove it.

About a dozen guys are playing catch and goofing around at the diamond farthest from the clubhouse. Must be Diamond A. Two or three of them are about my size, but most are quite a bit bigger. The coach is leaning against the dugout fence, his nose over a clipboard like he's solving a math problem.

The diamond's in good shape, the best one in the community club complex. I can tell right away it's a home run hitter's diamond. The fence in left field can't be more than eighty metres away. It's not even a real fence like we have in Jarvis Park, just one side of the boards of an outdoor hockey rink.

This city is so flat you can see for kilometres in every direction. From here in the outfield now I can see the downtown buildings standing grey and tall in the distance.

Black dirt, not sand-brown like we have in Toronto, lines the base paths. The pitcher's mound rises higher than what I'm used to in the eleven-year-old league. A tall pitcher on this mound would look like King Kong to the batter.

As I slice through the diamond, I take a quick look at my turf as a batcatcher — the area around home plate. Plenty of room between the plate and the backstop. Backstop's tall and solid. Not too many foul pop-ups can fly over it to stall a game. I could certainly get comfortable here. I cross my fingers and wish for the best. I hope these twelve-year-old Windsor Park Red Sox aren't too good for me.

When I step close enough that everyone can see I'm not just some kid passing through their diamond but a new guy about to join the team, all the players' heads turn to stare at me. I feel like you do when you're one of the last two kids being looked over by the captains in a neighbourhood game. I keep my eyes glued to the grass and trot over to the coach.

"I'm the new guy, Tom Poulos," I announce. I try to make this sound serious. All business.

The coach lifts his face from the clipboard and thrusts out his hand to shake mine.

"Coach Minuk, son. Glad to meet you."

His hands are strong and he shakes vigorously. When my father was alive, he used to say you could tell what kind of a person someone was from their handshake. I have a feeling this coach is testing me that way right now.

I pound my mitt a few times and wait for the coach to say something else. I take a good look at him. His brushcut makes his ears look big. He smells like aftershave lotion.

"By the look of that mitt, Tom, you must be a catcher," he says. "Tell me that's so because a catcher's exactly what we need around here if we're to make the playoffs."

I can't believe my luck. My heart pumps like a jackhammer. The rest of the guys are still playing catch, but their eyes are all over me.

"Yeah, I'm a catcher. Last year I played for the Jarvis Badgers. We made it to the City of Toronto semi-finals." I figure, why not throw that in? It can't hurt.

"Excellent. Our regular catcher, Frank Mitchell, is out of town for the summer. We have two games left this season and we have to win one to make it to the playoffs. That's not going to be easy considering both games are against the West Side Giants."

"I hope I can help," I say. Even though I'm super nervous, I try to sound professional. Baseball is serious stuff.

"I'm sure you can," Coach says. "Let me introduce you to the other guys." Coach funnels his hands around his mouth and shouts at the guys. "Come on in, men. We've got business to take care of."

He grabs a bat and ball from the canvas duffel bag flopped on the bench in the dugout. Just from the way he holds the bat, tightly around the neck and waving it with a flick of the wrist, I can tell he's a ballplayer. I've been stuck before with coaches who couldn't play ball and it's usually not much fun.

"This here's Tom Poulos," Coach says, pointing his bat at me. "He's a catcher and he'll be taking Frank's place behind the plate. Make him feel at home."

The guys don't appear too interested. But I know they must be underneath. That's the way it is when a new guy joins the team. You wonder if he's got what it takes. Anyhow, if I'm going to earn anybody's respect it's not going to be until I prove myself behind the plate or at bat.

"Let's start this off with some infield practice." Coach is barking now. "Starters, take your positions. Tom, you catch. The rest of you take the pitchers outside the third base line and warm them up."

I tool around inside the canvas duffel bag for the catcher's gear. First, I slip a brand new gold-coloured chest protector over my head, clasping it in the back. It fits loosely, but that's the way I prefer them to fit. The shin guards are old and falling apart. Some of the padding is spilling out. I pull them around my shins and fasten them. I grab a battered blue batter's helmet and place it on my head catcher-style, the bill facing back. Over that I draw the padded metal mask. It smells leathery. I look through the cage of the mask at the diamond in front of me and smack my new catcher's mitt to loosen it up. I smile. All of a sudden I feel like a real bat-catcher again.

Through the whole infield practice, I know the guys are testing me. Every time they hurl the ball at me they put everything they have on it. My palm stings from all the licks it's taking, but I don't miss anything. At one point I dive far to my right to nab a wild throw from the second baseman, which earns me a "Way to hustle, catcher" from Coach. I really appreciate that, because it means Coach is already beginning to think of me as his catcher.

I can tell right away that the best player on the team is the third baseman. And he acts it without showing off. He always knows what's going on all over the diamond. Something about the way he holds himself at third base, always leaning into the action, makes me like him.

After about a half hour of infield practice, Coach calls us all in around home plate. I start unsnapping my equipment. Some of the guys trot over and pat me on the back. I mumble "Thanks" back.

Then the third baseman, Kelly Myers, introduces himself. And am I ever shocked.

As Kelly shakes my hand and tells me I play well and will fit in with the team, he pulls off his green baseball cap. A mane of brown curly hair tumbles out and spills over the sides of his head and onto his shoulders.

Kelly Myers is a girl.

A girl!

"We're going to need your help against the Giants this Thursday," she says. Her eyes are green-blue, and her voice is confident and nice.

But I'm at a total loss. My tongue's hiding somewhere underneath my stomach. The best I can squeak out is a weak, "Yeah." I feel like a jerk. I think Kelly knows I'm shocked, but she just kind of smiles, then hits the bench for a cup of water. I stand there, stunned. I mean, I've seen girls play Little League before in Toronto, but I've never been on a team with one before, and I've sure never seen one as good as Kelly before. How am I supposed to act?

I guess normal, because Coach and the other guys don't seem to be treating Kelly special. Coach even calls the players "Men" or "Boys" and nobody seems to think it's funny. Kelly's just another player. Well, just another player who happens to be the best on the team.

As for the other guys on the team, it's funny, but some of them remind me of my teammates on the Jarvis Badgers. Not just their looks, but the way they act, too. Like Glen Arnason on second. He's a joker, the team clown. And he has this little nose dotted with freckles. Which is exactly like Victor Martin, the number one jester on the Badgers. These two guys could have been twins.

This is a new team, but in a weird way, even with the best player being a girl, it's not that different from what I'm used to. That makes me feel good.

But the good feeling doesn't last long. One of the pitchers, Jeff Foster, approaches me, and I smell trouble by the way he's staring me down — like he just caught me cutting through his yard. He's tall, and tight round muscles pop through the sleeves of his T-shirt. His blond hair's rock star long and wavy.

"Where you from?" he asks me, all snarly.

"Toronto."

"The big T.O., huh," Jeff growls. "Gonna play on the Toronto Blue Jays one day, Mr. T.O.?" He laughs then, as if what he just said is about as likely as snow on a summer day.

I stay silent. I'm not too bothered. I'm the new guy on the club and he's just having his fun. Rookies get ribbed, it's a law of sports. But something about this guy tells me he could go overboard. Fortunately, Coach is there to save me.

"Guys, you looked fine out there," he hollers. "Like a real team. But we need to work on our conditioning a whole lot. You're too slow and tire too easily to beat a team like the Giants. So let's line up for a quick sprint. Home plate to the outfield fence and back."

When Coach shouts "Go!" I take off as hard as I can, but I feel so nervous my legs might as well be locked in quicksand. Whenever I strain to make up a few strides, I seem to fall even farther behind the other guys. It's a losing battle. I'm not a fast runner, but I've never been last in a race before. Maybe there's just no way an eleven year old can keep up with twelve year olds.

I make it back to home plate last. Some of the guys are already sprawled on the grass catching their breath. I bend over next to Kelly trying to catch mine.

"Too slow, guys, much too slow," Coach yells.

I know he's not talking to me personally, but it feels that way.

"Especially our catcher," Jeff Foster mumbles under his breath, just loud enough so everybody can hear him. I feel like crawling into a hole somewhere and disappearing. Fast.

"Take it easy, Jeff," Coach says. "This is a team, not a collection of individuals. If we need to improve, we need to improve together."

Jeff makes a face and rolls his eyes.

"That'll earn you five push-ups, young man," Coach yells at him.

"I didn't say anything," Jeff protests.

"Five!" Coach shouts, pointing to the ground in front of Jeff.

"Just ignore him," Kelly whispers to me, nodding in Jeff's direction.

I hate a fuss like this. Especially when it's over me. Now for sure all the guys are going to hate me.

"OK," Coach continues. "Starters, take your positions in the field. Jeff Foster, you'll be pitching. Tom Poulos, you're catching. Everyone else line up to bat."

I'm worried about catching for Jeff. I don't know why, but this guy just plain doesn't like me. Some people are like that. They hate you the minute they set eyes on you. What if Jeff purposely throws wild pitches to make me look bad? No, he wouldn't do that. It'd make him look bad too.

I don't know what to expect. All I know is I have to play my best and earn the team's confidence. Even Jeff's. He's the main pitcher, and I'm his catcher. We have to get along. I know that. But I don't think Jeff does.

Coach calls the first batter, and I crouch down behind the plate, smacking my new catcher's mitt a few times for good luck. Maybe some of that Ernie Whitt magic will rub off on me.

The first guy up's Roger Frechette, the number two pitcher. Red hair spikes up from his head. His face is a freckle farm. He holds the bat awkwardly, like he doesn't enjoy being at the plate. I nod my head to give Jeff the signal to pitch.

I'm ready.

I wait.

Jeff's windup is real simple. He just steps forward with his left foot and lets go when his right arm flies past his ear.

But I can't follow the ball it's moving so fast. I'm secretly hoping Roger connects so I won't have to catch the ball.

I hold my mitt up in front of my mask, a wide open target.

*Slap*!

The ball lands right smack in the centre of my mitt. I feel it there before I see it. My palm stings from the blow.

Jeff can sure pitch hard, and like Danny Frankenheimer on my team in Toronto, he knows how to mix his pitches wisely. He boasts an efficient fastball, a tricky change-up and a nasty slider he throws with a sidearm delivery. His pitches move faster than what I'm used to, but I manage to stay right with them. If I hadn't already met the guy, I'd say it was going to be a pleasure catching for him.

Little do I know Jeff has a secret weapon up his sleeve. He brings it out when Mitch Friesen is up. Mitch has just fouled away three straight fastballs. I can tell Jeff is frustrated. He looks over at Coach as if asking for some sort of go-ahead. Coach nods his head up and down slowly and hops off the bench to lean closer into the action. I wish somebody would tell me what's going on. I bounce on the balls of my feet, ready for anything.

Jeff takes a whole lot of time preparing for his next pitch. The ball's hidden behind his hip.

What's going on here? My legs are so tensed I'm afraid if the pitch doesn't come soon I'll collapse.

Jeff winds up. But more carefully than usual. He doesn't kick his left leg out as far, but seems to be concentrating more on the way he's holding the ball. His body stretches out and his right arm is way behind, trailing the rest of him like a whip. As his arm comes down across his face, just as he's releasing the ball, I see his wrist flick around like he's turning a knob. As the ball leaves his hand, his index finger points straight out, like a pistol.

The ball hums straight for home plate, heading for the exact centre of the strike zone. Mitch brings his bat around and leans into the pitch. It looks like he'll connect. If he doesn't, the ball should smack right into my glove. I'm positioned perfectly. I've got my Ernie Whitt mitt opened wide and waiting.

But then, at the last split second, just as Mitch's bat is about to meet the ball, Jeff's pitch swerves way outside. I mean, that pitch changes directions like a getaway car making a hairpin turn. I can't believe it. I'm lost. It's all happened so fast and was looking so easy. My mitt's at least half a metre away from the ball's new path. I leap towards it, but with no luck. The ball has already passed me and is ricochetting off the backstop.

Mitch realizes I've missed the third strike and races for first base. I turn around, fling off my mask and chase the ball, but I'm so stunned I must look like a chicken with its head cut off back there. Finally I reach the ball, but Mitch is already at first. I make sure he stays put there, then toss the ball back to Jeff.

The expression on my face is, *What was that pitch anyhow?*

Jeff smiles. A big fat King of the Castle smile. So does Coach. He windmills his right arm and cries out, "Nice curve ball, Jeff. No way the West Side Giants are going to hit that."

A curve ball.

Jeff has just thrown me a curve ball.

And not some dinky little curve where you need a magnifying glass to detect the break. But a real live curve like they throw in the pros. In all the time I've been playing catcher, I've never had to handle a curve ball. Nobody on my teams has ever been able to throw one. But these are twelve year olds I'm playing with now. Their arms are strong enough to throw a curve ball. Trouble is, can I catch one?

Obviously not. Coach gives Jeff the signal to pitch the curve to the next two batters, and I spend most of my time digging missed balls out of the weeds growing against the backstop. Missed balls I should have caught if I was any kind of batcatcher. I'm embarrassed. I've slowed up batting practice. Coach finally moves in behind me to retrieve the missed balls.

Jeff keeps throwing his curve. I follow his muscled arm closely as he releases the ball, keep my eye on the ball as it travels to home plate, but I end up losing it at the last second. It's like trying to trap a fly in your bare hand.

Jeff seems to be enjoying my failure. He keeps looking at Coach with an *I told you so* expression. Like Coach should have known I was no catcher.

I miss yet another pitch and then feel a hand patting me on the shoulder. It's Coach.

"Look, Tom, don't worry about it," he says. "Jeff won't throw the curve much because it takes too much out of his arm. You did well behind the plate today. Why don't you take off your equipment and take a breather."

I walk off to the dugout, my head bent over like I've lost a coin in the dirt. I feel awful. I'm burning inside and my stomach is doing somersaults. I wanted to play baseball so badly this summer, but not here. Not in Winnipeg and not with these twelve year olds. And certainly not with a pitcher like Jeff.

# 4

# A Rainy Day

It's early the next morning and I can hear rain pelting the roof of the Olympic Diner. I've just woken up and my eyes are blurred from sleep. All night in my dreams I saw curve balls. One after another, streaming out at me like so many Tetris shapes I had to work my joystick to fit into place.

I half-sleepwalk to the diner in the front and find Uncle Nick in the kitchen, turning on the machines, getting ready for the day. I peek outside through the front door and see black clouds piled up on one another in the sky.

"Does it rain like this in Toronto?" Uncle Nick has followed me to the front door. He wraps an arm around my shoulders and looks up sadly at the dark sky, as if it were a sign of something. Something bad.

"Sure, sometimes. Even worse." I can remember at least a half dozen Badgers games that had to be cancelled on account of rain.

"It can't be good for business," Uncle Nick points out. "Nobody will want to go out to eat in this rain."

"Sure they will," I answer back.

Uncle Nick returns to the kitchen. He begins mixing the hamburger meat, and I watch because it's quite interesting. He flings a hunk of red ground beef into a deep metal pot. Then he adds eggs, chopped onions, salt, pepper, bread crumbs and olive oil, which he says gives the meat "a touch of Greece." He kneads everything with those thick strong hands of his. I can see he enjoys what he's doing. When everything's all mixed together, he places the pot of kneaded meat underneath a huge machine that looks like a giant corkscrew. The corkscrew spins the meat around, mashing all the ingredients together even more.

Then Uncle Nick gives me a job. He says I may be only eleven years old, but there's a lot I can do to help. That makes me feel good. Useful.

My job is to roll the mashed hamburger meat into balls and then flatten the balls into round patties. I roll the balls with my hands and flatten them with this other machine that looks like two cymbals attached at a ninety-degree angle. I put the ball of meat on the bottom cymbal and then squeeze the top cymbal down. That squashes the ball into a patty. If I use the exact same strength every time I bring the top cymbal down, the patties turn out identical.

I never knew that so much went into making something as simple as a hamburger. After a while my wrist gets sore. But I'm not worried. That soreness means the job is building muscle in my wrist. I hope my wrists turn out as big as Uncle Nick's. I need a lot of power in my wrists to hit and to catch Jeff's curve ball.

Uncle Nick's at the square chalkboard by the cash register, erasing last night's Dinner Special. "What are we going to put on special for lunch today, Tommy?" he asks me.

I haven't the foggiest idea. Since I've been at the Olympic Diner, everything I've tried has been great.

"How about roast turkey with gravy and cream of mushroom soup?" Uncle Nick suggests.

"Sounds good," I say.

"But we had that last week. Maybe lasagna, with Greek salad on the side?"

"Sounds even better." This is fun.

"Then again . . ."

The phone rings then.

"Can you get that, Tommy?" Uncle Nick asks me. He's lost in thought. His bald head's tilted up, and he's tapping the chalk against his chin.

"Sure," I say. I hurry to the phone. "Good morning, Olympic Diner. Can I help you?" I say into the speaker. That's the way Uncle Nick has taught me to answer the phone.

"Tom!" I hear my mom's voice clearly. "I see your Uncle Nick has put you to work already."

"I guess so."

"I bet it's fun."

"I guess so." I decide to give Mom the cold shoulder. I want her to know I still hold it against her that I'm not in the playoffs with the Badgers.

"Oh, come on, Tom. You're not going to make me feel bad about sending you away this summer, are you?"

"I guess not."

"It can't be that bad. If I know my brother, he's showing you a great time."

"He's nice."

"He's more than nice. It's better for you to be there, believe me. Toronto is so hot and humid right now. You can hardly breathe when you go outside."

"I guess so." My cold shoulder can get really cold.

"How's the baseball team?"

"Tough."

"Tough?"

"Well, I'm playing with twelve year olds, the only player on the team that's nice to me is a girl, and the starting pitcher throws a curve ball I can't catch."

"That doesn't sound too bad to me. You'll adjust." Mom can be *so* understanding sometimes. I don't say a word.

"Oh, come on, Tom. Everything will turn out OK," Mom continues. "Now give me your Uncle Nick for a few seconds. And don't worry so much. I love you, dear."

I call Uncle Nick to the phone. He starts talking Greek with my mom. I make out most of what he says. He tells her that everything's going great, that I'm no problem for him at all. Then he winks at me and turns back to the phone and tells my mom he wishes I were here all year long I'm helping out around the diner so much.

When he hangs up the phone, I thank him for putting in the good words. He laughs and says, "What are uncles for?"

At about eleven-thirty Vera shows up. She's wearing a yellow raincoat. She takes it off at the front door and tries to shake the water off. Most of it blows right back in, catching Uncle Nick and me in the face the way a yard sprinkler will when you pass one on the sidewalk. I lick at the drops of rain as they run down towards my mouth. That helps me wake up.

Vera slips an apron over her head and ties it around her waist. She's so thin she has to tie the apron strings twice around.

I go to the back of the diner and sit down on a wood crate to peel some potatoes. Uncle Nick taught me the proper way. You have to be careful not to peel too deep under the skin because Uncle Nick wants the Olympic Diner's fries to have a homemade look to them: big and fat and with some of the skin still on.

"You never did tell us how your first practice went yesterday, kiddo," Vera says. I like her, but I wish she wouldn't call me "kiddo."

"All right, I guess." What am I supposed to say? That I made a fool of myself trying to catch Jeff's curve ball? That I even thought of quitting? That I'd much rather be catching for the Jarvis Badgers than the Windsor Park Red Sox? Why did my mom have to do this to me?

"You like the team?" Vera asks.

"I guess," I say. "It's not going to be easy, though. Those twelve year olds are a lot faster and stronger than me."

"No they're not," Uncle Nick pipes in. "Remember, you're a Greek. The Ancient Greeks invented the Olympic Games. You spring from a race of great athletes. A Greek doesn't know what it means to give up."

"Yeah, right," I say. I get enough of that "Glory of Ancient Greece" stuff at Greek school. "You guys don't know how tough it is." I don't want to sound like a whiner, but I just have to tell someone my problems. "The starting pitcher, who doesn't even like me to begin with, throws a curve ball that looks like it's going one way, then all of a sudden curves in the opposite direction. There's no way I can catch that pitch."

"Sure you can, kiddo." Vera punches an imaginary glove in her left palm. "Just takes practice. Maybe I can help you out. I used to throw a pretty nasty curve ball myself when I was younger." Her right arm windmills like a softball pitcher's and she releases an imaginary ball. "Back when dinosaurs roamed the land."

I laugh.

Meanwhile, Uncle Nick is scratching the top of his head where the hair thins out into baldness. "What's a curve ball?" he asks, like he's totally lost in all of this.

I can't believe it. I mean, who doesn't know what a curve ball is? Why couldn't Uncle Nick actually be Ernie Whitt? Of course, what chance is there of a guy named Poulos having a relative who plays baseball? My friend Derek Boggs is always bragging about having the same last name as Wade Boggs. That must be neat, having the same last name as a big-leaguer. Too bad for me. The Greeks might have invented the Olympic Games, but I don't know of a single one who plays pro ball.

Just then a customer trudges in. His soaking wet galoshes make suction cup noises on the floor Uncle Nick has just mopped. By the time the customer sits himself down on a stool at the counter, Uncle Nick is already pouring hot black coffee into a cup in front of him.

"Well-done burger, easy on the onions, right Hank?" Uncle Nick asks.

"You get it right every time, Nick," Hank says.

Uncle Nick tosses one of the hamburger patties I flattened on the barbecue. Flames flicker up around the patty, and a rich hamburger smell fills the diner. It's like the warm smell of the burger overpowers the cold feeling of the rain outside.

"Business doesn't look too good, Nick," Hank says. "I'm sorry."

Uncle Nick doesn't say anything. Without even looking, he dumps a basket of french fries into a metal container that's under a hot lamp and shakes salt all over the fries.

Vera cuts in then. "Hank, you and a few other guys still come here for your meals, and we love you for it. But ever since that Super Burger opened up across the street, we've lost most of our customers. Everybody goes over there to eat now. It's the big new flashy place in the neighbourhood. What are we supposed to do?"

So that's why Uncle Nick was so uncomfortable when we had to go over to Super Burger — they're taking away all his business. Now it all makes sense. By the sounds of it, if something doesn't change fast, the Olympic Diner won't be open too much longer.

Uncle Nick finally says something. Not to anyone in particular, but just out loud. Kind of to himself, I guess.

"With Super Burger so close by, I might as well hang a CLOSED sign up in the front door." Uncle Nick's waving his burger spatula as he speaks. "Trying to beat Super Burger is like throwing a midget into the ring against Hulk Hogan."

"Don't worry about it, Nick," Vera offers. "They'll come back to you. The Olympic Diner's got the best burgers in town."

"I'll stick by you," Hank adds. He wipes a splash of mustard from the corner of his mouth. "I'll go down with this ship."

"Thanks a lot," Uncle Nick says.

"Hold on, we can take Super Burger on," I say. I'm not sure where this little pep talk of mine is coming from. "It'll just take a lot of hard work." Wow. Listen to me. I sound like my coach back on the Badgers.

Everybody in the diner laughs. It's like somebody turned the lights on in a dark room.

"My nephew from the big city is full of hope." Uncle Nick is behind me now, mussing my hair. "Like I used to be."

"I'm telling you," Vera says, "this little guy is going to be our good luck charm."

# 5

# On Base

A few days pass. I help Uncle Nick out at the Olympic Diner and worry myself sick about Jeff's curve ball. Then, before I know it, I'm at the ballpark for my first game with the Windsor Park Red Sox.

I'm nervous, no question about it. We're playing at home — on Diamond A — but I sure don't feel at home. I feel like a stranger on this team, like I don't belong. The rest of the guys are goofing around, pairing up to play catch until game time.

I stalk the dugout trying to look busy. My uniform doesn't fit right. It's too big and I have to roll up the legs of the pants. And I don't like the colour. I should be wearing the Badgers' blue uniform right now, not this ugly red thing.

It's a clear, sunny day. The bleachers behind the backstop are packed with fans wearing shorts and T-shirts. Most of them are parents of guys on our team, and every once in a while I hear someone shouting, "Attaboy, Mitch!" or "Knock it to them, Red Sox!" And the game hasn't even started yet.

The smell from the nearby meat-packing plants is strong today. Some of the Giants players are holding their noses, making fun of the neighbourhood.

Coach's wife, Mrs. Minuk, is sitting on a lawn chair just outside the dugout. She's wearing a baseball cap to shade the sun and holding Coach's clipboard on her knees. Her bare shoulders are sunburned. One by one she's calling the guys over to tell them their spot in the batting order.

When she calls me, I'm prepared for the worst. And the worst is what I get.

"You'll be batting last today, Tom, after Miles Hildebrandt."

I'm not surprised. I know I'm a decent hitter, but Coach doesn't know that. I should be happy I'm even playing right now.

We're up first, so I figure I'll have a chance to case the West Side Giants from inside the dugout. Based on what I've seen so far during infield practice, I'd say they're a crack team. And they look way bigger than our guys.

But I don't have a chance to stand around long staring at the Giants. Coach calls me out behind the dugout. He's waiting there with Jeff, his arm around Jeff's shoulders.

"Listen, boys," he starts, almost whispering to us like it's a football huddle. "I want Jeff to go the whole six innings if possible. Tom, help Jeff along, keep him paced so he doesn't tire out too fast. Jeff, I'd rather you didn't throw the curve today. The curve wears down your arm too fast. We'll use it only as a last resort."

What a relief! No curve ball to worry about. Now I can concentrate on the basics.

"Now warm up with a few pitches until you have to go up to bat," Coach tells us.

"Yeah, this eleven year old sure needs the practice," Jeff says.

I walk about fifteen metres away from Jeff and crouch down to a catcher's stance. Jeff doesn't say a word to me. I watch him closely, studying his pitching windup. As his batcatcher, I have to be totally in sync with him. Whether he likes it or not.

Jeff leans back now and lets go a fastball. It's so fast I don't realize it's coming until it's right in front of my face. I stick my mitt out to catch it, but not in time. The ball nicks the corner of the mitt and goes flying. Jeff shakes his head and rolls his eyes. I chase after the ball. It's rolled all the way into the outfield of a game going on in the far diamond. Some little kid there picks it up and tosses it to me. I feel like a twerp.

By the time I get back to Diamond A, it's already our turn to take the field. I clunk towards home plate with my shin pads slapping against my knees. I notice Uncle Nick in the grandstand behind the backstop. Even though it's hot outside, he's wearing that same green windbreaker he wore when he picked me up at the airport. He smiles at me and I smile back. I crouch down and fasten my pads.

The first batter up's a stocky guy with what I swear looks to me like a full moustache over his upper lip. He's all hyped up in the batter's box, not sitting still for a split second. When the pitch comes, he lets it pass and I can tell he was planning all along to sit on it.

The fact that he doesn't swing makes it easier for me to catch the ball. It's a strike that whips right into my mitt. With the ball in my mitt now I feel connected to the game, like a batcatcher again. This is what I was made to do. I love it. I carefully toss the ball back to Jeff, right at him so he doesn't tire himself out trying to catch it. I guess maybe I throw it a little *too* softly.

Jeff leans out to catch the ball with a sneer on his face. "What are you, a girl?" he screams loudly enough for everybody on the diamond to hear. I sit crouched behind the plate, thankful my face is hidden behind a catcher's mask. I can see Kelly over on third base, shaking her head from side to side. I wonder how she feels.

"C'mon, let's act like a team out here," she calls out to the whole infield.

The next batter connects on a lazy change-up, and then the whole Giants team really starts up the chatter. And one of the things they're saying is, "New catcher, guys, new catcher. We can take second easy. He's got no arm."

I'd like to say chatter like that doesn't bother me, but it does. I start thinking maybe I'll choke if I have to throw to second to beat a steal. I just hope the guy on first's too chicken to run.

Next batter's the Giants pitcher. He eyeballs me something nasty as he strides up to the plate. Jeff concentrates on him. If there's one guy a pitcher really hates to see get a hit, it's the opposing pitcher.

The Giants pitcher digs in for the pitch. Jeff must be a little rattled because he sends one skittering through the dirt. I fall to my knees to block the wild ball, but it takes a bad bounce in the dirt right in front of home plate and flies up straight into the air.

I throw off my mask so I can see the ball. The sun's sharp against my eyes and I have to squint. Finally I spot the ball. It's about four metres in the air and maybe three metres to my right. I race after it and nab it with my bare hand. The runner's already well on his way to second. I'm not even sure it's worth a throw, but I don't want to seem like a jam. I aim at Glen Arnason's target and let go. Not too hard, I admit, because I'm worried about throwing wild. The ball gets to second all right, but late. The runner's safe.

Coach calls out, "Good play, Tom, at least we kept the runner on second," but Jeff's giving me this look like, *Why couldn't you have thrown the guy out?*

The Giants pitcher is laughing now at the plate. He knows he's got Jeff flustered. Jeff does nothing to disprove him. The next three pitches are all balls, far out of the strike zone. The pitcher takes his base. Jeff shakes his head, frustrated.

I've played enough baseball not to lose my cool so early in the game. A lot can still happen. All we have to do is buckle down and get those last two outs. I'm hoping for the best.

Then Coach calls time out and strolls out to the pitcher's mound. All of a sudden I'm worried. What if Coach asks Jeff to throw the curve ball? I won't be able to catch it. It'll be a major disaster. Coach hasn't called me up to the mound but I scoot out there anyhow to find out what's going on.

"Look, Jeff, you just haven't found your rhythm yet," Coach tells Jeff, patting him on the back. "It's still early. Everything will fall into place. Just pitch to these next two guys, don't walk them. Your fielders will do the rest."

No curve ball. I breathe easier. Coach slaps me on the back lightly and says, "Way to catch, Tom. I like you behind the plate."

"He's no Frank Mitchell," Jeff mutters just as Coach and I take off from the mound.

The words feel like a stab in the back, but I keep walking back to home plate. I guess he thinks I'm just some eleven-year-old midget who's going to ruin his chances of winning the championship. As for Coach, either he doesn't hear Jeff's comment or he just decides to ignore it because he keeps right on for the bench.

I look up at the stands and see Uncle Nick. He's obviously been trying to get my attention. He waves at me. I don't think he even knows what's going on out here on the diamond, but there's no question he's rooting for me. That makes me feel better as I slip on my mask and crouch down behind the plate again waiting for Jeff's next pitch.

Everything happens so fast then there's no time to think: the bang of wood against ball, white ball against blue sky, ball cruising straight down like a missile. It's a foul tip high above my head.

I can hear shouts all around me but I can't make out what anyone's saying. My brand new Ernie Whitt catcher's mitt is turned up over my head waiting for the ball. I know I've done everything right — flung off my mask, positioned myself correctly, backed up my mitt with my right hand — but still I'm sort of surprised when I feel the smack of the ball against my mitt. It's there, all right. I hold on to that pop-up for dear life. Our fans cheer and so do the guys on the team. I see Uncle Nick up off his seat in the stands clapping his hands furiously.

I toss the ball back to the ump. Two out, one to go.

Jeff is back in stride. The team is really pumped up now, chatting him up, boosting his confidence. I helped him out there, and I hope he's thankful.

When it's our turn to bat, I take a few practice swings while the Giants pitcher warms up. I choose a wooden bat, not aluminum. I read somewhere that if you want to make the pros you have to get used to a wooden bat. And besides, I like the sound a wooden bat makes when it connects.

The bat I've chosen is a Barry Bonds model, size 30. It's light and feels good when I squeeze my palms around it tightly. I choke up a little because I like the control of a short choppy swing. I don't get many home runs this way, but I know I don't have the power to hit homers anyhow. I concentrate on placing my hits, peppering them around the infield for singles or doubles.

I march out to home plate when it's my turn up. Right now I'd just like to lay some wood on the ball and get things going. Neither team has scored yet.

But I can't concentrate. Because I'm with a strange ball club, in a strange park, in a strange city. I'm not myself. I can't help hearing the sounds in the ballpark. In fact, the cheers and jeers, especially the jeers, come at me like they're being pumped straight into my skull at an ear-splitting volume.

The first pitch flies at me like a blur. I try keeping my eyes on it, but my mind's wandering in a million different directions. When I swing, it's like a second thought. By the time I bring the bat around, the umpire's called out, "Stee-rike one!"

I step out of the batter's box to gather my thoughts. I tell myself to relax. I take a few deep breaths and concentrate on the task ahead of me: bringing that bat around to meet the ball. It's as simple as that. But all the fans out there, and Uncle Nick, and our team, and the opposing team, and the fact that I'd rather be playing on the Jarvis Badgers right now, all those things together make it so difficult.

The ump has to call me back into the batter's box I'm so dazed. I know I'm in trouble. My mind's wandering again. I'm thinking about what the pitcher's going to throw next, about what he thinks of me, about what my teammates will think of me if I strike out, about what I look like up at the plate. About everything but hitting that ball.

The pitcher goes up into his windup. I figure I'll bring my bat around early to increase my chances of connecting. I twitch at the plate, ready to swing. I hook that bat around fast. My eyes are closed and as I swing I realize I'm so separated from the game, from what's really going on now between me and the pitcher, that I wouldn't know whether I connected or not unless someone screamed it in my ear.

Next thing I know, the pitcher has thrown me a high and outside ball. I try to pull back, check my swing, but it's no use. I've already come too far around.

Strike two.

The Giants laugh. The pitcher's smirking at me. The catcher's tongue lets loose on a long razz: "No batter, no batter, no batter. Give 'im a pitch. Won't go nowhere but right here in my glove. No batter, no batter, no batter."

"Come on, you can do it," someone calls out from our dugout. I turn around and see it's Kelly. "Come on, Tom, start something off here. We need it." The way Kelly says that isn't just being nice. It's as if she really thinks I *can* get a hit.

That sparks something in my mind. It's like my mind's been this TV screen with poor reception and all of a sudden someone turns a knob and there's a perfect picture on it. I stride into the batter's box with confidence. I don't think about anything but that ball traveling from the pitcher's right hand to my bat. I block everything else out.

As the pitcher goes up into his windup, I follow his every move. I keep my eyes on that ball, and in my mind there's an invisible string connecting my bat to that ball. As the ball leaves the pitcher's hand I lock my eyes onto it. I follow it totally as it travels to home plate. I have no sense of time, of how long it takes that ball to get to home plate. My whole mind's concentrated on seeing it, on bringing the bat around to meet it. I wait for it patiently. Then, my eyes still on the ball, I press my bat around tightly. The fat of the bat just opposite the Barry Bonds signature meets head on with the ball. I see it meet the ball. I follow through with my swing and feel myself lining it over the third baseman's head.

I race for first. My head's down, and I'm smoking. Coach is on first, and he's giving me the signal to take second. I make the turn and rocket to second. I see the left fielder throwing the ball to the second baseman. I hear Coach yelling, "Slide! Slide!" My left knee automatically dips into a bend and my right leg pushes out in front of me. My butt hits dirt, and my right foot stretches for the bag. The second baseman's glove swerves towards my big toe. It's a close one.

"Safe!" The infield ump flings out his arms.

As I shove myself up off the ground and pat the dirt off my pants, I'm feeling great.

It doesn't matter that my legs are numb and my elbow still smarts from when I scraped it blocking home plate. The infield ump smiles at me and says, "Nice slide, kid." I reach into my pants pocket and pull out a dried fig. I pop it into my mouth for some quick energy. The second baseman looks at me like I'm some sort of nut.

Glen singles next, moving me to third, and Gord walks on four straight wild pitches. That brings Kelly up, with the bases loaded.

Kelly steps into the batter's box. She cuts the bat back and forth a few times, lining up her swing. She bounces her upper body lightly. She's ready.

I kind of expect the Giants to be razzing her because she's a girl, but they don't. I guess they've seen enough of her all season to know she's the real thing — a true ballplayer. Right now they're treating her like they would any other power hitter. The infielders fan out and the outfielders move back. Kelly stares the pitcher down. Her practice swings slice the strike zone in half. Her knuckles grip the bat tightly right above the end. No choking up for Kelly. She looks like an arrow pulled back all the way on a bow.

The pitch comes. I inch toward home. The ball's headed for the strike zone. Kelly's right foot pushes forward. Her shoulders twist. The bat meets the ball. There's a loud *crack*, and the ball rebounds off the bat. I race toward home. Everybody's eyes are on the ball. It's sailing over the outfield. The ball drops about twenty metres behind the rightfielder and keeps on rolling toward the street. I cross home as Kelly's rounding second. The hit's a sure home run. A grand slam. Glen and Gord make it home. By the time the ball's back in the infield, Kelly's already crossed home and being high-fived at our bench.

"Way to go," I tell her, after almost everyone else has congratulated her.

"You're the one that started it, Tom," Kelly says. "That was some double."

We trade skin. I show her a neat way of doing it I know from Toronto. You cross over and bang opposite fists together, then slap each other's palms. Kelly gets right into it.

I feel like I'm part of the team.

# 6

## The Team Chump

Coach tries to fire us up before we take the field for the bottom of the last inning. The score: Red Sox 5, Giants 3.

"C'mon, guys," he shouts, "hold on to this lead with your dear lives!"

We're raring to go, but we're not too sure we can hold on. I'm not, and I can tell the others aren't either by the expression on some of their faces. I guess they've been burned by the West Side Giants too many times before.

Jeff is rushing things up on the mound, like he wants the game over quickly so we can leave with the win under our belts. But it doesn't work. He's pitching wild, and I'm leaping all over the place like a frog on a stovetop, catching his pitches. The more riled he gets, the worse he throws. The first batter up blasts a triple off one of Jeff's fastballs. Then Jeff loses his cool and walks the next guy. I can feel the game being pulled away from us like that moment in an arm wrestle when you realize you're going down.

Coach calls a time out and hustles over to the mound. I move in to meet him and so do Kelly and Gord.

"We have to stop them," Coach whispers. "We can't let them get away."

"I wish I could just close my eyes and then open them and have the game be over and us the winners," Gord says.

"Well, it's not going to happen that way, boys."

"What can we do, Coach?" Gord asks.

Coach looks at me closely and then bites his bottom lip. "I think Jeff's going to have to throw the curve."

"No way," Jeff blurts out. "Poulos can't catch my curve. The Giants'll run all over us."

My stomach rattles. I keep my mouth shut.

"It's the only sure way to get them out right now," Coach says. "And I think Tom can do it."

"He couldn't at practice," Jeff exclaims. "We could sure use Frank Mitchell now."

"That's enough, Jeff."

"I knew we kissed the championship goodbye the second I first laid eyes on this Poulos shrimp. Why'd we have to let him on the team, anyhow?"

"Because he wanted to play baseball. That's as good a reason as there is."

"I still say he's going to make us lose. And you know it."

"And it doesn't matter, Jeff. Because Tom is our catcher and he's the one to do the job. Period. Can you do it Tom?"

"Yes," I say. But I don't think I can. Jeff's probably right. Right about now I wish I could just disappear.

"OK, guys, get out there and get them! Jeff, let her curve!"

Jeff turns away and starts rubbing the ball.

Gord pats me on the shoulder and says, "We need you, man."

Kelly says, "You can do it."

I shuffle back to home plate. My back aches and my knees are sore. We've been playing for over two hours now and my equipment seems to weigh a ton on my body. The straps are cutting into my skin. But I don't mind too much. It's all part of being a batcatcher.

I clamp my mask between my legs and put my helmet over my head. I check the stands for Uncle Nick, but I can't see him. I guess he had to get back to the diner.

"Play ball!" the ump yells.

I slip the mask over my head. I can smell the dirt and sweat on the padding. I crouch down and pound my new catcher's mitt a few times. Then I open that mitt up wide and offer up a target for Jeff.

A lot of good it does me. Jeff fires a curve ball that swerves away from the batter just as he's swinging into it. The batter tries to check his swing, but he's too far gone. So am I. I try to dive back, but the ball's already past me. It's a good thing the ball takes a clean bounce off the backstop. I catch it with my bare hand and turn around quickly to catch the runner trying to take second. He didn't expect to be running so he hasn't gone far. I cock my arm, and he returns to first. Next time I probably won't be so lucky.

Jeff winds up again. I know the curve ball's coming. I'm actually hoping the Giants batter hits the ball so I won't have to catch it. Let the fielders do the work.

I set my glove up as a target, but somehow know the ball's going to be nowhere near it. Jeff glides into his motion and uncorks another curve ball. The batter waits on it, trying to figure out how it'll curve. But he waits too long. By the time he decides to swing the ball's floating up and away from his bat.

He follows through on his swing as I stretch out to nab the ball. But I jump too high, and the ball crashes into my chest protector. I react as fast as I can, but the ball slips away from me and falls to the ground. The Giants coach screams at the batter to run. I've just dropped the third strike so he's free to take off for first. I pick up the ball out of the dirt and make my throw. The batter's bounding into first. At the same time the guy who was on third is heading home, and the guy who was on first advances to third. Merv catches my throw, but the batter's one step ahead of him. I see the ump's arms stretch out in the safe signal.

Red Sox 5, Giants 4.

They're closing in on us. Fast.

Jeff holds onto the ball and looks over at Coach. I guess he wants to know if he should keep going with the curve ball. Coach nods his head OK. My heart sinks like a yo-yo on its way down.

"C'mon, let's get two more outs!" Kelly yells from third base.

"They can't hit off you, Jeff," Gord calls out. "We've got 'em."

I hunker down and try to concentrate. I know I have to catch this ball. My eyes stay stuck on Jeff as his body heaves upwards into his windup. I'm as ready as can be. Jeff's arm comes down and hurls the ball. It's a curve ball all right, travelling fast. The batter pumps his arms and starts swinging. I'm just hoping the ball finds its way into my mitt. The bat slices the strike zone. But the ball rises a few centimetres as it crosses the plate, moving like a skipping stone. I push my mitt out into the ball. But it's still rising. The ball nicks my mitt and deflects into my mask. I feel a bang like somebody's plopped a tin pail over my head and gonged it.

The ball bounces about two metres in front of me, and I scramble for it. The runner on first is already on his way to second. I catch up to the ball and throw it as fast as I can. But I'm nervous now, embarrassed. The throw's wild, ending up way over Glen's head. The runner on third reaches home plate easily to score the tying run. The Giants scream out at the top of their lungs to celebrate their run. Jeff shakes his head angrily from side to side and looks over at Coach. It's only my first game with the Red Sox and already I'm the team chump. I hang my head and wish I could disappear into thin air.

My wish comes true. Coach calls a time out. Again he walks out to the mound, but this time his face is set in a frown. "Tom, I'm sorry but I'm going to have to pull you. Kelly, I want you to take Tom's place."

I feel awful. I don't know what I'm supposed to do now. "So do I take Kelly's place on third, Coach?" I ask.

Coach squeezes his eyes shut, then opens them. "Tom, maybe it's best you took a break. I'll call Roger in to take Kelly's place on third."

I'm out of the game.

Kelly follows me to the dugout so I can give her the catcher's equipment. We're both silent. I slowly take off the equipment and hand it over to Kelly. The mask, the chest protector, the shin guards.

It feels weird giving up that stuff, like it's mine and belongs to me and nobody else has any business wearing it. But I guess I don't deserve it right now. I watch Kelly slip on the equipment and a sick little worm eats through my insides.

I'm being replaced. And by a girl. I know that shouldn't bother me, because Kelly's probably the best player Coach has to replace me. But it does.

She's ready now, except for the catcher's mitt. I don't know whether I should lend Kelly my new Ernie Whitt mitt or let her use the beat-up old catcher's mitt in the team duffel bag. For a second there it seems like Kelly's reaching out for my mitt. But I don't make a move to give it to her. In the next second she's digging through the duffel bag for the old mitt. She pulls it out and gives it a few whacks.

"Sorry," Kelly says to me, ready to return to the game.

"It's OK," I say. "I hope you do well out there."

And then I yank off my mitt and hand it over to her.

"Use this," I say. "It's a lot better than that beat-up old thing."

"Thanks," Kelly says and smiles.

"Good luck," I say. Kelly runs out onto the field.

The umpire shouts, "Play ball!"

I sit down on the cold hard bench and feel light years away from the game.

And I never do get to see how Kelly does behind the plate. Because the Giants' next batter connects with Jeff's first pitch, another curve ball, just before it breaks, and whacks it over the fence in left field for a home run.

The Giants win the game, 7 to 5.

I sit alone on the edge of the bench and wish I had never come here.

# 7

# A Sore Loser

I guess I'm not a good loser. When my team loses a game, I don't like talking to anyone. If someone does try to talk to me, especially my mom, I just snap at them like a pit bull.

So when I walk into the Olympic Diner that night after losing the game to the West Side Giants, I'm not exactly in the mood for conversation. Problem is Uncle Nick's all excited over my first game and what he's seen of it.

"Tommy was great, Vera," he's saying now, his face alive, his arms waving. "You should have seen him. I don't even know baseball, but I knew he was playing like a star."

My head's still dragging, and I've got this mopey look on my face. Uncle Nick doesn't get the picture, but Vera does.

"Tommy, what's the matter? You look like you just lost the World Series or something. Your Uncle Nick here says you played an excellent game."

"We lost," I say, keeping it short and sweet. Or short and sour, actually. "I don't want to talk about it." That's when I take my Ernie Whitt catcher's mitt and fling it behind the counter.

"Tommy, you're going to lose sometimes," Uncle Nick says. "You should be pleased that you played as well as you did. I saw it with my own eyes. You were a real baseball player today."

"I played lousy," I reply. And I mean it. Why can't adults see the truth? "When it came down to the crunch, I failed. I couldn't catch Jeff's curve ball. I didn't belong on the diamond."

"You tried your best, I'm sure," Vera pipes in.

"Well, I guess my best wasn't good enough."

"That's no way to talk, Tommy," Uncle Nick says. "You're putting too much pressure on yourself. Losing's part of the game. Next time you'll do better."

I plunk down hard on one of the stools at the counter.

"Your mother called while you were at the game, Tommy," Uncle Nick says. "She said to call her back as soon as you were done."

"Maybe later," I say. The last thing I want right now is to speak to the person responsible for sending me up here in the first place.

Uncle Nick moves away from me then and crosses through to the kitchen. "Let me make you one of my special burgers. It'll make you forget all about losing."

If only it was so easy, I think.

Uncle Nick tosses two hamburger patties on the barbecue. Then real fast like one of those TV cooks, he chops up some mushrooms and onions and throws them on the grill to sizzle.

"Wait until you taste this, Tommy," he says, grinning. "Vera, anything for you while I'm back here?"

"How 'bout an order of french fries. I haven't eaten much tonight."

I can't believe this. Personally I feel like running away to my room and never seeing anyone again. I don't want to sit and eat and chat with everyone. Right now Uncle Nick is a bother to me. Vera is a bother to me. The Olympic Diner is a bother to me. And most of all the Windsor Park Red Sox twelve-year-old baseball team is a bother to me.

I have no business on that team. I'm not twelve years old and I don't live in Windsor Park. I don't even live in Winnipeg. I live in Toronto, Ontario. And I'd like to be there right now.

"I think I'm going to my room right now." I say. "Uncle Nick, I'll just pass on that burger."

"You just played a game and you must be hungry," Vera says. "Stay here with us for a while and have Uncle Nick's burger. Maybe you'll feel better."

By then Uncle Nick has already cooked the burger and placed it on the counter in front of me. I am hungry so I figure I'll just stay and have the burger. But I sure don't think it'll help me feel any better.

I sit down next to Vera, who's jabbing her fries into a puddle of ketchup, and take a few bites. Uncle Nick must be real proud of the burger he's made. He hovers over my shoulder a few seconds watching me eat, making sure I like it. The burger really is tasty. The two patties are smothered in fried onions and mushrooms. Chili sauce is dripping out the sides.

As Vera and I continue eating, Uncle Nick goes to work cleaning out the french fry fryer. He does this every night after dinner. He empties out the used-up oil through a special filter into a tin pail. The oil gushes through a long tube at the bottom of the fryer. You can see little bits of burnt fries spill out with the oil. They get caught in the filter. The rest of the oil seeps through to the pails. I watch this whole process now kind of mindlessly, not because I'm interested, but because there's nothing better to do. Like reading some goofy magazine in the waiting room of the doctor's office.

When I'm done my burger, Uncle Nick walks up to me and puts his arm around my shoulder. "Not a bad burger, huh, Tommy?"

"Yeah."

"Anything else I can get you. Some pie for dessert, maybe? Vera baked an apple pie this morning, tasted so good I had two pieces already."

"I can see that," Vera jokes, pointing at Uncle Nick's round stomach.

"No thanks, I'm full," I say.

"Come on, Tommy. Cheer up. You did your best. That's the important thing. Winning or losing, you really have no control over that. You can't worry about the things you can't control."

"Who cares anyhow?" I say. I'm still in no mood for a lecture.

Uncle Nick then takes off his apron and tosses it into the laundry hamper at the end of the kitchen. He comes back holding a baseball in his right hand. I have no idea what he's up to.

"Tommy, if you'd like, we can go outside and practise. So you're more prepared for the next game. Maybe I can help you."

He's got to be kidding. If I practise with Uncle Nick I'm liable to get worse, not better.

"No thanks."

"Come on, Tommy. Just you and your Uncle Nick out in the parking lot. I'll throw you some balls, and you can practise catching them. I'll try to make them curve for you."

Then I say something I shouldn't say. I know I shouldn't say it, I know I'll feel bad later about saying it, but I still say it. It's like I have to. Like my feeling so lousy about losing, about being here in the first place, is my excuse to make somebody else feel lousy.

"You don't know the first thing about baseball, Uncle Nick. You can't help me."

"Tommy," Uncle Nick says, like he's begging me to take back what I just said.

"I wish I had never come here," I say.

"Please don't say that."

"Leave me alone!"

Uncle Nick's face stiffens. Slowly he moves to the coat rack and grabs his windbreaker. He opens the front door and steps outside. He doesn't go anywhere, just stands there at the entrance with the baseball in his hand.

I realize right away I don't feel any better for taking that jab at Uncle Nick. For trying to make *him* feel bad. In fact, now I feel even lousier.

"Are you happy with yourself?" Vera says. I know she's mad.

"No," I say. I'm not lying.

"That's no way to treat your uncle. He's going through a very tough time right now with the Super Burger opening up across the street and taking away all the Olympic Diner's customers."

"I know."

"No, you don't know. You don't know that this morning the manager from Super Burger came over here wanting to get your Uncle Nick to sell the Olympic Diner so they can expand their parking lot. You don't know that Uncle Nick just might sell because he needs the money. And that would mean the end of the Olympic Diner, which is his pride and joy. You don't know that Uncle Nick came back from your game today saying how much it helped get his mind off his troubles. How happy he is that you're here and that you're playing baseball."

"I'm sorry." That's the best I can say right now. I feel worse than ever.

"I'm sorry, too, Tommy. I don't want to come down hard on you. I know it's been difficult for you having to come up here this summer. Just try to give your Uncle Nick a chance."

I sit there, staring at the wall. Vera goes on, "Tommy, I don't have any real family. My husband left me eleven years ago, and we never had any children. Your Uncle Nick, and the regular customers here at the Olympic Diner, they're my family now. And you, too."

Vera sips at her coffee. The steam mists her eyes. She looks tired. I walk to the front door. I don't feel like going outside right now. I feel like crawling under the covers in my bed at home and blocking out the world. But I'm not at home. I look outside the front door for Uncle Nick. He's sitting alone on a cement bench at the side of the diner. It's dark outside and the white of the baseball in Uncle Nick's hand seems to glow. He's tossing it in the air and catching it as it falls. He does this again and again. The Olympic Diner sign is flashing on and off, the gold lights blinking on top of him. The lights going on and off are like a clock ticking. Uncle Nick seems to be tossing the ball up in time with the ticking. I turn back and head straight for my room.

# 8

## "Quit the Team!"

The next morning when I wake up and make my way into the diner for breakfast, Vera is there alone, sipping some coffee and nibbling away at a plate of hash browns. The newspaper's open in front of her, but she doesn't seem too interested in it.

"Where's Uncle Nick?" I ask.

"He's still out in the back. I went in to check on him when I opened up this morning and he said he wasn't feeling very well, that he'd probably take the day off."

"Do you think he's still mad at me?"

"He's not mad, Tommy. I guess he's just disappointed. He thought spending this summer with you would be a lot easier than it's turned out to be."

I feel awful just then. Real low. It's like I just can't win. Either something rotten happens to me or I do something rotten to somebody else.

I have no appetite for breakfast, so I just take a seat on an upside-down crate behind the front counter and start peeling potatoes. Vera tramps back there with me and loads the dishwasher with dirty plates. We both work pretty much silently, just kind of staring out into space.

I work my knife around the potatoes like a professional barber cutting someone's hair with scissors. In no time I've filled up a whole pail with peeled potatoes. For a while at least my mind is totally off baseball, totally off my next game with the Windsor Park Red Sox, and totally off Jeff's curve ball.

Until the front door of the Olympic Diner bursts open and in walks Jeff Foster himself, with two friends I've never seen before. All three of them are wearing oversize black and silver L.A. Kings sweatshirts with matching baseball caps. They head straight for the pinball machine in the far corner of the diner. Jeff spots me just as one of his friends starts up a game by whacking the machine hard on its side.

"The guys said I'd find you here," he says with a sniff.

I guess someone on the team found out I'm staying at my Uncle Nick's for the summer. I don't know what to do. I don't want Jeff to think I'm hiding behind Vera or anything, so I walk out to the pinball machine. I'm kind of embarrassed. I'm wearing a full-body white apron with stains all over it and I'm holding a potato in my hands. Meanwhile, Jeff and his friends look like they just walked out of a jeans commercial. They must think I'm a real loser. I wish I could just hide.

"Hey, Mr. T.O., you work here or what?" Jeff says this loud, like he's trying to get the attention of his buddies. But they're totally into their pinball game.

"Yeah, I work here," I say. "This is my uncle's place. I'm staying with him over the summer."

"So this dump is your uncle's, huh," Jeff says. "Should've figured it."

Vera can't hear any of this over the noise from the dishwasher, which is just as well because if she kicked them out or something right now I'd feel even more embarrassed.

"Hey, guys," Jeff turns to his buddies again, "this is the kid Coach found to take Frank's place on our baseball team."

One of the guys twists away from the pinball machine and gives me a quick once-over. "You've got to be kidding," he says. "He's not even half Frank's size." Then he turns back to the pinball machine.

"I know," Jeff laughs. "And he's not much of a ballplayer, either. We could have had Kyle Nesbitt to replace Frank, but there wasn't room after this bozo signed up." Then he looks me right in the eyes. I want to move my glance away, but he's locked right on me, like he's not bothered by this at all. "And if he knew what was good for him," he continues, not so much to the other guys, but actually right at me, "he'd quit the team! Retire."

"What's that supposed to mean?" I say. I feel a drop of sweat trickle down my nose and onto my upper lip. It stings.

Jeff moves in closer to me. His face is only a few centimetres from mine now, and I can make out how it's turned a shade more red. "I want to win the championship this year. Bad. The last thing I want is for some eleven-year-old runt from Toronto who can't even catch a curve ball to ruin it for me. You're not good enough for our team. Get it?"

I don't say a word. But I'm burning inside. And wishing this eleven year old from Toronto was right back there where he belongs. Toronto.

Jeff is spitting out his words now. "If you know what's good for you, you won't show up for our next game." He shoves his hands deep into his pockets, and as he does his right elbow spreads out and jabs me in the shoulder. I don't know if he meant that as a shot or not, but he's looking at me right now like he's saying, *So what are you going to do about it, kid?*

I can feel tears pushing at my eyes, but I hold them back. I'm just hoping Vera hasn't seen or heard any of this and decides to break it up, because it'll make me look like a suck.

Then one of Jeff's friends starts bashing the pinball machine really hard. "Hey, this old thing just ate up my two quarters!"

Vera does hear this and moves over quickly to the three boys. She pushes the coin return button on the game, but nothing comes out in the slot underneath. She's looking over the machine trying to figure out what went wrong.

"Are you sure it ate up your quarters?" she asks. "We've never had a problem like that with this machine."

"Yeah, I'm sure," the kid says. "Are you calling me a liar?"

"No," Vera says. "Let me just get two quarters out of the till myself and see what happens."

"Forget it," the kid says.

"Yeah," Jeff adds. "Let's get out of here, guys. Across the street at Super Burger they've got these brand new video games that are really awesome. I don't know why we even came to this lousy joint in the first place." He dirty-looks me. "Don't forget what we talked about," he says in a low voice.

They storm out and slam the door behind them. Vera shakes her head and mutters, "Kids nowadays," then kind of chuckles and says, "Ooops, sorry kiddo. I didn't mean you, of course."

I take a deep breath and wipe away at my eyes. My hand comes back moist. Maybe Vera can laugh about this, but I can't. A hundred thoughts are swirling through my mind at the same time, and my stomach's flipping all over the place. Part of me wants to quit just like Jeff wants and the other part of me wants more than anything else to show him that I'm a good baseball player who can help the Windsor Park Red Sox win the championship.

I don't know what to do. I tear off my apron, chuck the potato in my hand at the kitchen wall, and race back to my room.

# 9

# Kelly Myers

The first thing I do when I'm in my room is grab my catcher's mitt and smack it a few times, just to let off some steam. I'm mad, mad at Jeff, but I'm scared, too. The reason I came to Winnipeg for the summer instead of going to camp was so that I could play baseball, and now the pitcher on the team thinks I'm so lousy he's trying to scare me into quitting. What am I supposed to do?

I decide to take a break from the diner and just be alone. I head for the ballpark, lie down on the green grass and gaze up at the clouds in the sky. Jeff's threat inside the diner is like a bad dream that keeps running through my mind, pushing everything else out. All I can think about is quitting.

Playing baseball in Winnipeg just isn't worth the trouble. Why should I be struggling right now to learn how to catch a curve ball? I was just fine on the Badgers catching fastballs and change-ups and sliders. Why couldn't it stay that way? And how am I going to play in next week's game if Jeff doesn't want me there? Maybe I'd be better off if I just didn't show up. I mean, who'd miss me? In fact, maybe Jeff's right, maybe the Windsor Park Red Sox would be better off without me.

I'm lying here throwing a ball up in the air straight above my head and catching it in my Ernie Whitt catcher's mitt when it falls back down. When you have no brothers or sisters, you learn to do a lot of things alone. This is how I play catch alone.

I keep tossing the ball up like that and catching it, but not concentrating at all. The grass is cool against my back, but the stench from the meat-packing plants is really strong today and my nose feels plugged with it.

I miss my pals in Toronto. I miss the Jarvis Badgers. I hate the fact that I have to spend almost a whole summer here. Quitting the baseball team's probably my best bet.

In the sky white clouds form all sorts of shapes. I stare at a cloud every few seconds and make a game of coming up with a half dozen things it might be. I guess you'd call what I'm doing right now daydreaming. But it's as close to fun for me as anything else I can do in this town.

"Hey, Tom!"

I look around in the direction of the voice and spot Kelly Myers. She's on a bike with a canvas bag full of newspapers draped across her body. Her brown hair is loose around her shoulders. In her right hand, she's holding a wax cup with a thick straw sticking out of it. I notice smudges of grape slurpee on her lips.

"What's going on?" she asks. "You looked like you were daydreaming or something."

I'm embarrassed. The one player on the team I like and who maybe likes me back and I act like a goof in front of her. My palms start to sweat.

"I guess I was daydreaming," I say. I don't feel like lying.

"I daydream a lot, too," Kelly says to me, like daydreaming's the most normal thing.

"It's fun. Sometimes it's so much fun I don't want to snap out of it."

"Like in science class when the teacher's blabbing about something boring," I say.

"Or when your mom's yelling at you and you couldn't care less," Kelly adds. We laugh.

Kelly hops off the bike and sits down next to me. She holds out her slurpee to me and says, "Want a sip?"

"No thanks," I say.

Then she notices the ball and mitt that I've dropped at my feet. "You're a pretty good batcatcher," she says.

"Thanks," I say. I'm glad to hear her say that. "But Jeff doesn't seem to think so." I wonder if I should tell Kelly about Jeff's threat.

"Jeff's got a problem, that's all," Kelly tells me. We start lazily tossing the ball back and forth. It's fun to play catch with someone again. She brushes her brown hair back out of her eyes. "He thinks he's the star and the rest of the team are a bunch of guys he has to live with. I guess he figures because you're only eleven and not too big, you're not a good player. He thought the same thing about me when I first tried out for baseball last year. I remember how he just stared at me and made faces all during the first practice, until I whacked one of his pitches over the outfield fence. I like winning, too, but I don't get so hung up about it that I make it tough on everyone else on the team."

"I guess we had a player like Jeff on my team back in Toronto."

"There's a player like that on every team. Except the winning ones. Jeff tries to bully off the team anybody he thinks isn't as good as him. He doesn't realize that, before long, there won't be anyone left on the team but him."

I decide to tell Kelly about Jeff's threat. "Actually, Jeff came by and told me I'd better quit the team. He said he had a friend who would be a better catcher. Maybe he's right."

"No way!" Kelly says. Her green eyes are sharp and intense. "He's trying to scare you, but he won't do anything if you stick it out. You're just going to have to prove him wrong. Last year, when I first wanted to sign up for the boys' team, a lot of people tried to make me quit, including Jeff and even some parents, but I kept right at it. I really wanted to play, that's all."

"So do I. More than anything else."

"So don't quit. Just ignore Jeff."

"I can't ignore his curve ball, though," I say. "I don't know if I'll be able to handle it."

"Coach doesn't let him use it too much," Kelly says, "because it's hard on his arm. You'll do OK."

"I hope so."

"Don't worry, Tom. You looked good behind the plate to me. We *need* you."

"I guess so." I laugh. I'm glad Kelly showed up right now. I decide right then and there I have to stick it out. I want to play baseball. I want to play baseball more than anything else this summer. Even if it is on the Windsor Park Red Sox.

"How'd you get so good at baseball, anyhow?" I ask. I'm not trying to be rude or anything, it's just that I really want to know. I mean, it's not every day you meet a girl who can out-bat, out-run and out-throw most boys on the team.

"My older brother's really into sports," she says. "Right now basketball's his favourite. He's always shooting baskets at the hoop my dad put up over our garage. When he was into baseball, I kept hanging around him until he let me practise with him. Mostly, I just liked catching a ball with a glove. It felt good. It really was as simple as that. Before long I think I was just as good as him. When I joined Little League, I didn't want any fuss or anything, just to play baseball. There's no girls' hardball league around here."

Kelly is staring at the sky, and I wonder to myself if she's looking at the clouds the same way I just was, trying to come up with things they look like.

"I guess the teams in Toronto are real good, hey?" Kelly says.

"They're pretty good."

"Do you ever go see the Blue Jays play?"

"I've been to lots of Jays games. The Skydome's not too far from where I live."

"Must be something. The only pro ball I see is on TV."

"Oh, I love it at the ballpark. There's always something to watch. One inning I'll just look at the batcatchers, see how they do what they do. Next inning I'll concentrate on the pitchers. Each time it's like a whole new game."

"I'd love to go see just one game."

"If you're ever in Toronto, I'll take you."

As soon as I say that, I kind of wish I didn't. It sounds too much like I'm asking Kelly out on a date or something. But I did mean it. It'd be fun to have Kelly visit me in Toronto.

"I wish I could play Little League in Toronto," Kelly says then. "You probably even have pro scouts come out to your games. I mean, the Blue Jays are *right there*. Who's going to notice me here in Winnipeg?"

"You'd like to play in the big leagues?"

"Sure would," Kelly says. Her green eyes stare ahead as if she's looking far into the distance. "I have this dream that I'll be the first girl player ever in the major leagues. They'll put me on the cover of all the sports magazines. Everybody'll be talking about that great girl on third base."

"I have a dream a lot like that, of making the majors. I want to catch for the Jays."

"My dream probably won't come true."

"You mean because you're a girl?

"Yeah. They'll never let girls play in the majors."

"You never know," I say. Kelly loves baseball so much I feel bad she thinks her dream can't come true.

"Yeah, you never know," she says.

Talking with Kelly now is a lot of fun.

"Why are you in Winnipeg, anyhow?" Kelly asks.

I honestly don't know where to begin. Do I tell Kelly about how my dad died two years ago and left us alone? Do I tell Kelly that my mom thought I was too young to take care of myself during the days when she was away at work? Or that my Uncle Nick suddenly decided it was time to meet his nephew?

"Have you ever heard of a place called the Olympic Diner?" I say.

"Heard of it?" Kelly says. "I practically grew up on Olympic Diner burgers. My dad used to bring home burgers from there every Tuesday night. That was the night my mom didn't have to cook. But now we go to Super Burger. My little brother cries if we don't go there."

"Well, my uncle owns the Olympic Diner," I say. "That's why I'm here in Winnipeg. I'm spending the summer with him. I'm supposed to help him out."

"Mr. Nick is your uncle? No way!" Kelly says this like it's something special to have Uncle Nick for an uncle.

"Yeah, he's my uncle."

"He's sure a nice guy. Last year when we were studying Ancient Greece in social studies our teacher took us to the Olympic Diner and Mr. Nick bought the whole class french fries and showed us these slides of ancient statues and temples that he took when he visited Greece."

I smile. I could see my Uncle Nick doing that. I feel a sharp pain suddenly in my chest over the way I treated him after the game.

Kelly hops back on her bike. "I've got to get going," she says. "I have to finish delivering these newspapers."

"See you."

"Yeah, see you," she says. "Maybe I'll come by the Olympic Diner and call on you one day so we can play catch."

"Sure," I say. I'm not sure if she means it or not. But I hope she does. I need a friend here in Winnipeg, and I think Kelly would be a real good one. And, besides, playing on the Windsor Park Red Sox, I'm going to need all the practice I can get.

I push myself up off the moist grass then and watch Kelly as she rides her bike through the field, her legs pumping the pedals hard, her long hair floating in the wind.

# 10

# "You Can't Give Up!"

Over the next few days Uncle Nick and I keep our distance. I help out at the Olympic Diner, peeling potatoes, pressing patties, sorting out the stock room, taking out the garbage. But I stay out of Uncle Nick's way. And I get the feeling he's staying out of my way. Like he's not so sure he made the right decision asking my mom to send me here this summer. Both Uncle Nick and I use Vera to communicate with each other. If he wants me to do something, he usually tells Vera and then she tells me. If I want to ask for permission to do something, I ask Vera and then she just kind of looks at Uncle Nick and he nods his approval. It's not that I'm still mad at Uncle Nick, because I really don't have any right to be, it's just that I'm ashamed of myself for being so mean to him after my first game and I'm not sure how to face him.

It's weird, but now that I've been hurt too, by Jeff, I realize more than ever just how much I must have hurt Uncle Nick the other night when I told him I didn't want his help. I have to let Uncle Nick know I'm not going to let him down again. Enough giving him a rough time, enough blaming him for my problems.

And then, I get an idea.

Suddenly, as I'm staring absently at some hamburger balls I'm pressing into patties, with Vera chopping onions beside me and Uncle Nick sleeping in the back room, I get an idea. I get an idea that'll make my Uncle Nick happy and make my stay in Winnipeg a lot more fun. My mind's like a TV screen with this idea fast-forwarding over it. I see it all: how I'll pull it off, how it'll happen, how happy it'll make Uncle Nick.

I'm going to save the Olympic Diner. That's right. I know just how. Just how to make everyone realize the Olympic Diner's food is a hundred times better than Super Burger's. Just how to get everyone back eating at the Olympic Diner so Uncle Nick can stay in business.

There's no way I'm going to let them turn the Olympic Diner into more parking lot space for Super Burger. Now that I've worked with Uncle Nick, helping him make his special hamburgers and his homemade french fries, I know how much better the Olympic Diner's food is than Super Burger's. It's just more *real*. The trick is to make the old Olympic Diner customers see that.

And I know just how to do that.

A taste test.

I'll call it the Great Burger Taste-Off. The Olympic Diner versus Super Burger. Uncle Nick's best burger against theirs. Let the people decide.

The awful feeling I've had over treating Uncle Nick so poorly is like a heavy weight on my shoulders that I can't wait to let down. I want him to know I'm not a bad kid. I want to make up with Uncle Nick so much that I decide to go wake him up. I tiptoe into his place in back of the diner and peek into his room. He's lying on the bed with his eyes closed, but it doesn't look or sound to me like he's sleeping. When Uncle Nick is asleep, you can hear it. He snores as loud as a windstorm. Now he's silent, his arms folded behind his head, his feet crossed at the ankles.

On his dresser, there's a stack of books. I can tell they're library books by the white tags at the bottom of the spines. I read the titles on the spines and see that they're all books about baseball. I guess Uncle Nick has had to turn to books to learn about baseball. That's how much of a friend I've been.

"Uncle Nick?" I say, quiet enough not to wake him if he's asleep, loud enough so he'll hear me if he's awake.

Uncle Nick wags his head the way you do first thing in the morning when you splash water on your face, then lifts himself up off the bed.

"Tommy, what are you doing here?" he says, sitting on the side of the bed, rubbing the heels of his hands into his eyes. "Did Vera send for me? Is the diner busy?"

"No, Uncle Nick, everything's OK up front," I say.

Uncle Nick's eyes are groggy, and his cheeks and jaw are dark from not shaving. He's wearing one of those sleeveless undershirts and I see his biceps bob as he puts on a shirt. I'd love to have arms like that one day.

"I guess I just feel lazy today," Uncle Nick says. "What's the use of getting up and going to work anyhow? Maybe I should sell the diner, Tommy. What do you think?"

I feel like telling Uncle Nick about my plan to save the Olympic Diner, but I hold back. I want it to be a surprise. But I do want to say something right now, something that'll make him feel better.

"Your burgers are the greatest I've ever eaten," I tell him. "The people will figure it out."

"You really like my hamburgers?"

"No kidding," I say. "You're a great cook."

Uncle Nick smiles and neatens his moustache with a brush of his fingers. "I think maybe it's time I started teaching you a few tricks at the grill," he says.

"I hope so," I say. I know we've made up now. I feel that same relief I do whenever Mom starts talking to me again after she's grounded me or sent me to my room. "I want to learn all your secrets. Your burgers are a hundred times better than Super Burger's."

I guess I shouldn't have mentioned Super Burger, because all of a sudden Uncle Nick's face goes gloomy like a shadow's passing over it.

"Tommy, I just don't know what to do," Uncle Nick says. There's no trace of anger over the mean things I said to him that night after the game. He's talking to me like I'm his best friend. "I never bothered anybody, Tommy. Twelve years ago, I took over the Olympic Diner, worked hard to make it the best restaurant I could, to serve the best food I could, because that's all I wanted out of life, and now ... I can't understand it. Here, I've been telling you not to give up, to practise hard and learn how to catch the curve ball, so you can play with the twelve year olds, but in my own battle, I've already given up. And I know I couldn't do otherwise. Because sometimes your opponent is just too much for you."

"No!" I say, loudly. "You can't give up!"

And as I say that *No*, I realize I'm saying *No*, to Uncle Nick, *don't give up your fight against Super Burger*, but also I'm saying *No*, to myself, *No, I won't leave Winnipeg until I learn how to catch a curve ball*. Jeff or no Jeff.

Uncle Nick puts his strong arms around my shoulders and pulls me close to his chest. I don't pull myself away. He's warm and I can feel his heart beating fast against my ear. I hug him back. And it feels good. All of a sudden I see what it really means for Uncle Nick to be my uncle. We're family.

"We can beat Super Burger," I say.

There's a knock at the door then, and Vera pokes her head inside. Uncle Nick bends down to slip on his shoes, fancy black leather dress shoes he wears everywhere, even in the Olympic Diner kitchen.

"Sorry to bother you boys," Vera says. "But there's some-one here to see Tom."

"To see me?" I ask, and scrunch up my face like I couldn't imagine who it could be.

"Yes," Vera says, and winks at me as if she doesn't want Uncle Nick to see. "I think it's one of your friends from the baseball team."

# 11

# A Deal with Uncle Nick

When I get back into the Olympic Diner, I can't believe who's waiting for me there, sitting on one of the swivel stools at the front counter. It's Kelly, and there's a baseball glove shoved between her arm and her side, and her Windsor Park Red Sox cap is bill-back on her head. I'm glad she's kept her promise to call on me.

"Hi," I say.

"Hi, Tom. How you doing?"

"Not too bad, I guess," I say.

Kelly pulls her glove out and slips it onto her left hand, then smacks it a few times. "I was wondering if you wanted to practise with me," she says. "We have a big game coming up."

I don't know what to say. I'm really excited I have someone to play catch with and maybe work on some drills with. I've decided there's no way I'm letting Jeff stop me from playing on this team.

"We can toss the ball around in the parking lot outside," I suggest.

"Sounds good to me," Kelly says. The gum she's chewing blows out into a bubble and snaps. "Let's go before it gets dark."

The sun is just starting to set out behind the meat-packing plants, like it's a round hunk of dark cheddar melting into the earth. Across Frontenac Street at Super Burger cars are lined up at the drive-thru intercom and further up teenage workers are leaning out the pick-up window handing out bright bags of food. Kelly and I line ourselves up away from where Uncle Nick's Riviera is parked in front of the diner.

We just play catch for a while, throwing the ball back and forth easily, getting comfortable with one another, and then we try some harder drills, like what each of us might face in a game situation. I throw Kelly some grounders, and she whips some pop-ups high into the air for me.

All of a sudden I wonder whether Kelly might be able to help me learn how to catch Jeff Foster's curve ball. I figure, why not ask her?

"I don't know, Kelly," I say, "no matter how much I practise with anyone, how am I ever going to learn to catch Jeff's curve ball?"

Kelly shakes her head. "I wish I could throw a curve ball," she says, "but I can't. If you could only practise with Jeff, maybe you'd get better at catching curve balls," she adds. "Too bad, I doubt that'll happen. But you're a pretty good ballplayer, Tom. I know that. Maybe you can't catch Jeff's curve ball, but there are a lot of other things you do that we really need."

"Thanks," I say.

Then Kelly says, "Hold on, there's something I want you to try out." She walks over to where the huge garbage dumpster is at the side of the Olympic Diner and shuffles through some used cardboard boxes until she finds one about the size she's looking for. Then she walks to the far side of the building and sets the box against the brick wall there, so that the open end is facing me.

"An important part of being a batcatcher is being able to throw to second base, right?" she says. "Not just catching the pitcher's throws."

"Right."

"Good," Kelly continues. "What I want you to do is start down from a squat and then pop up as fast as you can and throw the ball at that box. Make believe it's second base. If you get the ball in the box, and fast, it means you get the runner out. If you practise with this box now it'll be the easiest thing in the world to throw to second base in a real game."

I like Kelly's idea. And I could certainly use the practice pegging off baserunners trying to steal second.

"Sounds like a good drill," I say. "Let's get started."

Kelly trots back to the box, and I start throwing at it.

I miss my first five throws.

Kelly is there to catch the ball and hums it back to me. She's cheering me on, urging me to keep trying. I keep trying.

I start getting a few balls in the box, and Kelly and I both whoop it up. We've got a rhythm now, me throwing the ball into the box and Kelly fishing it out and chucking it back. I get on a roll and it's like I can't miss that box. Kelly and I are counting out loud how many throws I make. I'm up to twelve and I'm having a great time. By the looks of her, Kelly is too.

We practise like that until I've made twenty-two throws. I think we're both exhausted by then. We've really practised hard. We sit down on the pavement. The cool cement feels good against my legs. It's getting late now and you can hardly see the sun behind the meat-packing plants, only the swirls of colour it's throwing — orange, pink, red — into the grey clouds in the sky.

I decide to tell Kelly about my idea to save the Olympic Diner.

"My Uncle Nick's in trouble, you know," I say. "He might have to sell the Olympic Diner. All his customers are eating at Super Burger now. Just like your family, I guess."

"I can't believe it. I mean, I just figured the Olympic Diner would always be there."

"No. Actually, the manager of Super Burger has offered to buy the diner from my Uncle Nick. He wants to turn it into a parking lot."

Kelly shakes her head. "That's too bad."

"But I'm not going to let that happen," I say.

"What do you mean?" Kelly asks.

"Well, I've been spending a lot of time thinking about this, about how I can help my Uncle Nick, I mean really help him, and I've come up with this idea. I think it's a pretty good one."

"Let's hear it."

"OK." I'm excited about sharing my plan with Kelly. "I call my idea the Great Burger Taste-Off. I'm going to set up a little booth on the street between the Olympic Diner and Super Burger. I'll buy five burgers from Super Burger and get five burgers from the Olympic Diner. I'll cut up the burgers into small pieces, and lay out one piece of each for people to taste. I'll do it at lunch time when there'll be a lot of people around. I'll ask people to choose which burger is the best. I know they'll choose the Olympic Diner's. Everyone'll see that Uncle Nick's burgers are the best. That Super Burger's just a big company with a lot of TV commercials. Word'll get around, and the Olympic Diner's customers will come back."

"I like it. I can paint a banner for you. I'll write THE GREAT BURGER TASTE-OFF on it, and we'll hang it across the front of the booth. That way nobody will miss it and everyone will be curious to see what the booth's all about."

"We'll wrap the burgers up in aluminum foil to keep them warm, and offer the people free pop."

"Yeah. And I'll call up all the newspapers in town and tell them what's going on. My mom works in the accounting department at TV 5. I'll ask her to tell the reporters at the station what we're up to. Who knows, maybe they'll send one."

"And we'll make a huge scoreboard where we write out how many people choose the Olympic Diner's burgers and how many people choose Super Burger's."

"And I'll get my dad to help us build the booth."

"This just might work, Kelly."

"This *will* work, Tom. I know it will." We trade skin the way I taught her at the game.

"Uncle Nick'll be so happy. We won't tell him anything. I don't want anyone knowing about the Great Burger Taste-Off until it happens."

Just then Uncle Nick comes outside. "It's getting dark. I'm going to turn on the sign," he says, lifting his chin to the Olympic Diner sign. "Can I bring you two back some orange juice?"

"Fine," I say. I look at him and can tell he's happy I seem to have made a friend.

"No thanks, Mr. Nick," Kelly says. "I've got to get going. I still have to collect from my paper route."

Kelly pushes herself up off the pavement and hops onto her bike, which is resting against the wall of the Olympic Diner. "See you at the game, Tom. Let's hope we can beat the Giants this time."

"See you," I say. We share a secret smile then, like we've both got our fingers crossed that the Great Burger Taste-Off will work.

"Good night, Kelly," Uncle Nick says.

"Good night, Mr. Nick."

Uncle Nick starts to walk back to the diner. I watch him and I watch the neon sign in front of him, its lights out now, not blinking, the colours in the letters of OLYMPIC DINER kind of washed out, waiting to be turned on for the night.

Uncle Nick goes inside and in a few seconds the Olympic Diner sign is lit up. I can't help staring at it, the way the letters seem to dance on and off, the way the little torch flickers. If you look hard enough, you can see that the torch isn't actually flickering, that it's just one horizontal line of lights after another lighting up, from one end of the flame to the other, and then all over again and again. It's weird, but just as soon as you look at the flame long enough to make out each line of lights, all the lights suddenly blur together, and the flame looks like it's actually flickering again no matter how hard you try to make out each line of lights.

While I'm daydreaming like that, I hear Uncle Nick's shoes clopping on the cement. I turn my head and see him returning with two wax cups of orange juice.

"How was your practice? Did you practise catching a curve ball?"

"No," I say, "only Jeff Foster can throw those. But we had a fun practice anyhow. Kelly sure is a good baseball player."

"I could tell," Uncle Nick says, and smiles. "She's really good at picking up those grounders."

"Where'd you learn about grounders?" I ask.

"From those books I've been reading," Uncle Nick says. "I've done a lot of research. I bet you'd be surprised."

I have to admit I'm kind of impressed. The only reason Uncle Nick has tried to learn about baseball is so that he can talk about it with me.

"It's been interesting," Uncle Nick goes on. "And I've learned a lot. For example, I bet you didn't know that one of the best batcatchers ever was a Greek."

"Yeah, right," I snicker. He's got to be pulling my leg now. "You're going to try to tell me Johnny Bench was really Greek? Or Ernie Whitt?"

"No. But Gus Triandos was. He hit thirty home runs for the Baltimore Orioles in 1958. You can look it up."

"I believe you," I say, and laugh. "You got me." I mean, *Gus Triandos* sounds just as Greek as *Tom Poulos*. I guess you don't have to be named Boggs or Bench to make the big leagues.

"Maybe you can make the record books yourself someday," Uncle Nick says, picking up the cardboard box. "It's about time there was another Greek batcatcher."

A pile of litter blows across the parking lot then and Uncle Nick bends down to pick it up. He takes a long time doing it and is looking closely at the litter. Then I see why. The litter is a bag and a styrofoam hamburger container. From Super Burger. They're that bright blue and yellow that Super Burger uses on all their paper bags and packages. Uncle Nick crunches it all up into a ball. I figure he's going to go over to Super Burger and throw that garbage right in the manager's face. But he doesn't. He just takes it to the big aluminum garbage can at the side of the diner and drops it in.

"It's like the Olympic Diner is already gone," Uncle Nick says to me as he walks back. He's shaking his bald head from side to side. "What can I do, Tommy?"

"Give it your best shot," I say. Then I remember that Uncle Nick gave me about the same advice a few days ago, and I was stupid enough then to get mad at him. I hope he doesn't get mad at me, now.

"You're probably right," Uncle Nick says, sipping his orange juice. "But I think that this time even my best won't be good enough."

"Let's make a deal," I say.

"What kind of deal?" Uncle Nick asks.

"I learn to catch a curve ball, and you keep the Olympic Diner open no matter what."

"That's some deal," he says.

"Isn't it fair?" I say.

Uncle Nick's eyes bunch together like he's thinking. His moustache curls up. Then he smiles.

"Yes, Tommy, it's fair. You be the best batcatcher you can be, and I'll be the best cook I can be."

"It's a deal," I say.

We shake hands and I try to squeeze inside Uncle Nick's strong hand like a man. Then he takes a folded piece of paper out of his wallet. He unfolds the paper and stares at it a few seconds.

"You know what this is, Tommy?" he asks.

I shake my head no.

"It's an offer from Super Burger to buy the Olympic Diner. All I have to do is sign it, and the Olympic Diner is theirs." Uncle Nick's voice cracks, kind of like he's crying, but also kind of like he's laughing. "They want to turn us into a parking lot. That's why the manager there has been so nice to me."

I don't say anything. I don't think there is anything for me to say right now. Seeing Uncle Nick so upset makes me feel awful, but I'm also secretly hoping that my Great Burger Taste-Off idea will work. I want to remind everyone what they're missing by not eating at the Olympic Diner.

And then, under the glimmer of the gold and orange lights from the Olympic Diner sign, Uncle Nick tears the piece of paper into as many little pieces as he can and throws the pieces into the cool night air.

# 12

# Making the Playoffs

At the game the next day, it's cloudy, and everyone's looking up at the sky, praying those clouds don't turn dark and start raining down on us. Both teams want to play this game. Both teams think they can win.

I pair up with Kelly, and we start playing catch, while the West Side Giants take the diamond for infield practice. It's so much better than last game, when I felt so alone. Now Kelly and I play catch as though we've been playing catch together before games all season long.

Jeff's not pitching tonight because Coach is saving him for the championship. If we make it. When Jeff sees Kelly and me playing catch, he stops to watch us, hands on his hips. "Oooh, you two are real friends, all of a sudden. This wouldn't be love now, would it?"

"Give it a break, Jeff," Kelly says. Not angrily, just matter-of-factly. "We've got a baseball game to win today, remember?"

"Touchy," Jeff says. "That's the first sign."

"Of what?" I ask. This is too much. I don't see why Jeff has to be smart-alecky about Kelly and me being friends.

"Lay off," Kelly puts in just then. "If you just opened your eyes you'd see that Tom's been hustling for this team ever since he joined. And that if we want to win the championship we can sure use his bat at the plate."

Jeff ignores Kelly and looks directly at me. "All I can say is, *you'd* better not screw everything up for us today. Then you'll really wish you'd listened to me." He glares at me then, long and hard. Finally, he jogs back to our bench.

Personally, I'm just glad to turn my attention back to the game ahead of us. If we can't beat the Giants today, we can kiss the playoffs goodbye. We haven't beaten them all season long, but everyone on the Red Sox seems to think we can win this time. I guess because we came so close last game.

Do the Giants *ever* think they can win! Out on the field they're practising loosely, hot dogging around as if they don't have to take us too seriously. This is their home field, and the players are showing off for their fans. They're acting like they've already won the game, talking about the team they're likely to meet in the playoffs, the Forest Park Cardinals.

That's all the better. If they don't want to take us seriously after last game, that's their problem. We're here to play today.

Mrs. Minuk calls me over to let me know my place in the lineup. I trot over to her on that lawn chair and peek at the sheet on her clipboard. I can't believe it. Coach has moved me into the lead-off position. After my four-for-four showing last week, he must be confident that I can get the hits. I'm not planning to disappoint him. Jeff is still batting clean-up. Coach has pulled Merv and put Jeff on first. Roger Frechette is pitching and batting last.

The lineup on Mrs. Minuk's sheet looks like this:

1. Tom Poulos C
2. Glen Arnason 2B
3. Kelly Myers 3B

4. Jeff Foster 1B
5. Gord Yamoto SS
6. Joey Brown LF
7. Miles Hildebandt RF
8. Mitch Friesen CF
9. Roger Frechette P

When I walk out to the plate in the bottom of the first inning, I can feel the eyes of all the fans on me. The Giants fans are just as loud and cocky as the players. I wish Uncle Nick were here to cheer for our side.

I move into the batter's box, ready to swing. I do my best to concentrate, to keep my mind on the pitcher and the ball. The pitcher's a new guy we didn't see last game. He's a lefty. His name's Wes Weschuk. Lefty's are always scary up on the mound.

The pitch comes at me, and it looks good. I pump that bat around and swing my body into the pitch. But at the last second the ball breaks and swerves away from my bat.

It's a curve ball.

It's also strike one.

I step out of the batter's box and look around. Kelly's standing up in the dugout, rooting for me.

"Go on, you can hit this guy!" she shouts.

I step back into the batter's box, waiting for another curve ball. Sure enough, the next pitch is a curve, but it breaks too soon. I hold back and watch as it swerves outside the strike zone.

Ball one, strike one.

I know this guy can't throw curves all night, or his arm will go out on him in two innings. I figure the next pitch should be a straight-ahead fast ball. I figure right. I swing at it and connect. But the ball sails foul over our dugout.

Ball one, strike two.

I'm in trouble now, but the key is to stay cool and concentrate.

The pitcher tries another curve. The ball boomerangs way inside for another ball.

Ball two, strike two.

Now I'm ready. I'm staring that pitcher down like I know I can hit his next shot. He hums a change-up at me, but I wait it out, and it crosses the plate fat and juicy as a pumpkin.

I swing. I drive my legs and shoulders into the ball, directing all my strength into the meat of the bat.

*Bang*!

I connect. The ball sails over the shortstop's head and lands about a metre in front of the centrefielder. He runs towards it, but the ball takes a high bounce right over his head. By that time, I've crossed first and am heading for second. I make it standing up.

The guys on our bench scream out in celebration. They're on their feet, hooting and hollering. Coach Minuk windmills his right arm. The fans are clapping. I guess I put on a good show for everybody.

At the plate now, Glen is more than ready, like my hit has really pumped him up. The pitcher throws him an inside ball, but Glen steps back and golfs it, way over the first baseman's head. I race home and score an easy run, while Glen reaches second base.

The guys on the bench are shouting, "Rally! Rally!" as they pat me on the back. Coach Minuk has a fat smile on his face. The West Side Giants coach, dressed in sweats and a tight T-shirt, stomps his feet in disgust.

Kelly is up next, and she wants a part of this rally. She digs in at home plate and arcs her body back waiting for the pitch. The Giants pitcher releases what looks like a curve ball. Kelly jumps on it, meeting the ball a split second before it curves. The ball booms off the bat deep into right field. Glen clocks around the bases with Kelly following him. Screaming at the top of our lungs, the guys and I in the dugout are up off the bench. Glen makes it home, and Kelly holds at third.

Windsor Park Red Sox 2, West Side Giants 0.

The Giants fans fall silent in the stands. Their coach stalks up and down the baseline. I think he'd like to get out there and do the pitching himself. He's barking orders left and right. The guys on the field feel bad. You can tell by the way they hang their heads. Mrs. Minuk lets out a loud giggle and says, "They're cracking! Boys, I do believe the West Side Giants are finally cracking!"

"You bet they're cracking," Glen adds. "We're going to make scrambled eggs out of them tonight."

At the end of the first inning, we're up 3 to 0. As we move into the middle innings, Roger is a thing of beauty on the mound. Sometimes a pitcher will get up there and just take control of the game. Like it totally belongs to him and he can do with it exactly as he pleases. Roger pitches now in an easy, rapid rhythm, and I try my best to help that rhythm along. I don't drop any of his pitches. I'm doubly careful that all my throws back to him sail right into his glove. When a pitcher's on a roll like Roger's, the catcher's best bet is to just make sure nothing happens to disturb him.

The Giants just can't get a hit. One by one they come up to the plate and one by one they strike out, pounding their bats into the dirt all the way back to the bench to show their frustration.

In the bottom of the fourth, Kelly and I sit together on the bench and study Weschuk's delivery. We look for little signals he gives when he's about to throw a certain pitch. We try to figure out the best way to hit off him. I'm having a great time. I even offer Kelly a dried fig, and she tries it, no questions asked. And loves it! I can't wait to tell Uncle Nick.

The fourth inning ends with the score, Windsor Park Red Sox 5, West Side Giants 0. We're totally pumped. All of us, Coach included. But we're not taking it easy or starting to joke around. And nobody's even daring to say anything like, "We've got this in the bag." It's like we're afraid to jinx ourselves. I wish Uncle Nick were here to see this, but I can't spot him anywhere in the stands.

The Giants ready themselves for their fifth at bat. They've made a few changes, and we're seeing some new faces up at the plate. The clouds up in the sky are getting blacker and blacker. A huge shadow has swallowed the diamond. Everybody's eyes are on the sky. If it rains now, before we've finished the fifth inning, the rule book says the umpire has to call the game. Nobody wins. We'll have to play it all over again.

The first Giants batter of the inning strolls into the batter's box. His teammates aren't so much rooting him on as rooting the clouds on. They'd sure like to see some rain right about now. The sky rumbles and the clouds swell. The Giants are running around in the dugout like they're performing a rain dance. But there's no rain.

When our at-bat comes, I get another hit, a line-drive triple that bounds deep into right field. From third base, I take a look back at our bench and see Kelly clapping wildly. I can make out Jeff, too, looking at me kind of funny. I can't say for sure whether he's impressed or disgusted. Not that it matters, anyhow. I know I've really panned out as a batter. In two games here, I'm now seven for seven.

We finally make it through the fifth inning, and the rain has held off. Coach Minuk takes a deep breath. As we're about to hit the field for the top of the sixth, he yells, "Let's finish these guys off now."

As the Giants prepare themselves for their last at-bat, their coach yells at them. He's telling them off for everything they've done wrong. Everybody can hear him.

"Go out there and win back this game," he shouts. "If you guys lose, you're all staying right here after the game for a practice. Nobody's going anywhere!"

A practice right after the game. That coach is crazy. But he's got his team fired up. Their bats get hot. Nobody can blame Roger. He's still pitching the same as he was in the first inning. It's just that the Giants are hitting different. Better.

And they're mean now. Out for blood. I don't think they want to practise tonight.

Before we know what's hit us, the Giants have scored three runs.

Red Sox 5, Giants 3. Only one man's out, and the Giants clean-up hitter is up. There's a guy on first, revved up and ready to take second.

As the clean-up hitter saunters to the plate, I stand up to stretch my legs. They're tired from squatting all day. I feel like tiny pins are stuck into the backside of my knees. I take a look through the stands, and my heart jumps when I see Uncle Nick. He's made it to the game, after all. He's holding that baseball of his in his right hand. I smile at him.

The umpire yells out "Play ball!" and I crouch down behind the plate again. A line of sweat has formed where the padding on my mask touches my face. The sweat trickles down into my eyes and the salt burns them. I'm praying our two-run lead holds.

Roger releases a fastball. The clean-up guy's all over it. The hit splits the infield. The runner on first reaches third while the clean-up guy settles in at first.

I look out onto the field and don't like what I see. With one out, the Giants have a runner at first and third. That means the runner on first'll probably try to steal second, figuring we won't want to risk throwing him out just in case the runner on third takes home. This is the worst position for a catcher to be in.

Coach T's his hands into a timeout signal and calls the infield and me out to the pitcher's mound.

"Look, guys, we can't let the Giants get away from us now. Not when we've done so well so far."

"That's right," Kelly says.

Coach looks at me. "The ball's in your court now, Tom. I can guarantee you that guy on first is going to try to steal second on the next pitch. If you think you can throw him out in time to keep the runner on third from racing home, I'm going to call a pitch-out play."

I think about that one. I look over at the runner and then I look at second base. I remember the practising I did with Kelly, throwing the ball straight into that cardboard box that was supposed to be the second baseman's glove. I made twenty-two of those throws that night. I figure I can make another one right now.

"I can do it," I say to Coach, as well as to the other guys.

"Good. Here's what we're going to do. Roger, you pitch the ball high and outside. But fast. The runner's going to take off the second the ball leaves your fingers. Tom, you jump up and out and grab that ball. Then whip it to second. Don't even watch it. As soon as you've thrown the ball, turn around and block home plate from the third base side. That runner'll be coming home. Glen, you tag out the runner from first, then whip the ball back to Tom. Kelly, you back up Tom at home. Let's go!"

I can feel my pulse pounding through my body. I turn around and head back to home plate. Uncle Nick's still in the stands, sitting on the edge of his seat. So's everybody else out there.

As nervous as I am, I have to admit I'm also thrilled. This is an exciting game, as exciting as any game I've ever played in Toronto with the Jarvis Badgers. A game like this is why I love baseball so much.

I crouch down. I keep my glove centred in the strike zone so the Giants don't figure we're pulling a pitch-out play. The runners on first and third inch off their bags, but the way Roger stares them down keeps them from taking too much of a lead.

I concentrate on second base. I stare at the bag until I've stared so hard it looks like that cardboard box I was throwing at in the Olympic Diner parking lot. Roger winds up and throws. Both runners start moving. I bound up and nab the ball a metre in front of the batter. I'm not going to let him block me. I let loose immediately. I keep my eyes on the bag at second, all the time seeing it in my mind as that box I was throwing at in Kelly's drill. It's a perfect throw, low enough so that all Glen has to do is catch it and his glove is right on the sliding runner's feet. Meanwhile, the runner from third is hurtling home. But Glen is already releasing the ball, another perfect throw about a metre in front of home plate on the third base line. I'm there to catch it, and the runner puts the brakes on.

The throw's about three paces ahead of the runner. He's caught in a hot box. I hold onto the ball, and Kelly moves forward a few steps. We work together like a real dynamic duo. I hold onto the ball until the runner turns back towards third. Then I unleash a quick throw to Kelly. The runner's a dead duck. He just collapses a metre in front of Kelly and Kelly tags him out.

We've won! And beating a team like the West Side Giants makes the victory all the sweeter.

Our guys run in and throw themselves on top of Roger. The West Side Giants are gathered around their dugout, gazing at us with stunned expressions. Their coach is having a cow, yelling at the guys to take the field for their practice. Coach Minuk comes over and shakes all our hands. He's beaming. I look into the stands and see Uncle Nick on his feet, his arms outstretched in celebration. He's shaking that baseball of his in his right hand like it's a good luck charm.

When the shouts and dancing have settled down, Kelly walks up to me and pats me on the back.

"Great game," I tell her.

"Wasn't it! It feels great to beat those guys."

"Sure does."

"You helped us out a lot. I'm glad you ended up here this summer."

"So am I."

"Are we still on for tomorrow?"

"You bet. Operation Great Burger Taste-Off is set to begin."

# 13

## The Great Burger Taste-Off

It's a morning of clear blue skies three days later when Kelly and I are supposed to put my Great Burger Taste-Off idea to work.

I make my way to Kelly's. Her house isn't too far from Uncle Nick's place, but it's in a newer area, farther away from the meat-packing plants. The streets are quiet, without all the noisy trucks blowing out black smoke that drive by the Olympic Diner. There are no sidewalks, just huge green lawns. Most of the houses are medium-sized with attached garages. I spot Kelly's house by the official NBA backboard over the garage. That must be where her older brother practises all the time.

The garage door is open and I see Kelly inside, hunched over a battered old work horse putting the finishing touches on the banner she promised she'd make. It's really something. Bright green letters announce, "THE FIRST ANNUAL GREAT BURGER TASTE-OFF." I admire it a few seconds and I can see that Kelly's happy I like it.

I think Kelly is as excited about saving the Olympic Diner as I am. It's amazing all the things she's done for me. We're using her dad's work table as a booth, and she's spiffed it up with new paint. She even has a clean red-checkered tablecloth ready to spread over it.

"OK, now, let's go over our plans again," I say.

"Have you brought the scoreboard?" Kelly asks me.

"It's right here." I pull out the scoreboard from an old gym bag I've brought with me. On one side of a huge sheet of white poster paper I've drawn the letters OLYMPIC DINER, with gold letters and an orange torch, just like the sign. I've used felt markers. On the other side I've drawn SUPER BUR-GER, in bright blue letters. I have a black felt marker with me to mark off the people's choices.

"How about the money for burgers?"

"Right here," I say, patting my pockets. Lucky my mom gave me some cash for this vacation. "Have you called the newspapers?"

"I've called both newspapers and told them this was going to be a big event and they should send a reporter," Kelly says. "And my mom promised to tell the newsroom at TV 5 about us."

"Great!"

"Let's set our watches."

We set our watches. It's eleven o'clock. One hour to showdown.

"We leave here as soon as possible," I say, "and carry the booth out to the boulevard between Super Burger and the Olympic Diner. I'll set the poster and scoreboard up. Then I buy five regular hamburgers from Super Burger and you buy five regular hamburgers from the Olympic Diner."

"Got you."

"That should take about ten minutes, tops," I continue, "Then we're ready to really get started. We'll carefully slice up the five hamburgers from each place into twenty pieces and lay them out on the booth."

"Then it's up to the people."

"Exactly."

"Maybe we should get started?"

"Let's go."

And we do. We're like two secret agents in a spy movie. We both know what we have to do. I feel good knowing someone like Kelly, a real winner, is helping me out. My fingers are crossed hoping everything will work out.

Just as soon as we set up the booth, people start gazing our way. All the drivers in the cars passing by slow down to take a better look. I guess we're some sort of attraction. Exactly as planned.

At a quarter to twelve Kelly and I leave the booth to pick up the hamburgers. I look back and see Kelly's banner waving in the wind. It looks great. I'm nervous. I'm also scared. We're not doing anything wrong, but for some reason I think someone's going to stop us. Going to tell us we can't hold the Great Burger Taste-Off.

When I walk inside Super Burger, I get even more nervous. It's as if I walk into a freezer. My spine tingles, and the skin on my arms turns prickly. There are too many bright lights, too many people. The floor seems to be sloping up and then down. I'm dizzy. I want to turn back.

But I know I can't. I take a few deep breaths and come back to my senses. I walk up to the ordering counter. There's a long lineup, but it's moving fast. I keep my head down and my shoulders hunched so that nobody notices me. I feel like I'm about to stick the place up or something.

I place my order with a blonde girl who must be around fourteen. I ask for five Super Burger "Soops." That's what they call their regular hamburgers. Then I look behind the girl to watch the hamburgers being prepared.

But nobody prepares them. I've never stopped to think about it before, but at Super Burger the burgers are ready when you make your order. There's no barbecue, no Uncle Nick cooking the hamburgers. Instead, all the hamburgers are stacked in neat rows behind the ordering counter inside styrofoam containers. There's a big yellow light over the hamburgers to keep them warm. The girl just grabs the hamburgers from the stacks and hands them to the customer.

I'm wondering now where those hamburgers come from. While the girl's putting my Soops away in a fancy blue Super Burger paper bag, I gaze around looking for a barbecue or a grill or something. What I see is a long conveyor belt like they have at airports for your luggage, only narrower, and the hamburger patties rolling down this belt to guys and girls who slap on mustard, relish, ketchup and Super Burger's secret sauce. Everybody's super fast at what they do. They work like robots.

I pay the girl and take off with the bag. My heart's racing, and I keep hoping everything's going OK with Kelly. I'm hoping Uncle Nick hands her the five best "Olympians" — that's what he calls his regular hamburgers — ever to leave his barbecue. I'm hoping this idea works.

When I get outside, I run back to the booth. Kelly's not there yet, and I don't see her coming either. There's no time to waste, though. I start cutting up the burgers and putting little pieces on separate paper plates, the ones Kelly and I have written "Super Burger" on the bottom of.

As I'm cutting, Kelly appears, with a plain brown bag from the Olympic Diner. She quickly takes out the Olympians and cuts them up into pieces the same size as mine. Gradually, people are starting to gather around us, asking us what we're doing. It's a beautiful day so almost everyone from the meat-packing plants has come out for lunch. Most people are headed for Super Burger, and only a few people are walking towards the Olympic Diner. That's what we're trying to change. When people ask, "What are you kids up to?" we tell them. Soon we're stopping everyone who passes and inviting them to try our taste test. Most people exclaim, "All right! Free food!"

Before long, there's a lineup of people waiting to take the taste test. First up is a young woman in a red dress. She's joking with her friends. I show her the two plates. She doesn't know which plate has which restaurant's hamburger. She reaches out for the hamburger on the plate to my right. She chews it slowly, making a big act of it. "Not bad, not bad," she says, when she's swallowed the burger. Then she takes the other hamburger and places that in her mouth. Right away her eyes light up and I know this is the burger she's going to choose. Her mouth's full of the hamburger and she's rolling her eyes upward. She says, "Uhm, uhm, uhm."

"Ladies and gentlemen," Kelly begins, like she's a barker at the circus. "Our first participant has completed the taste test."

I offer the young woman a cup of pop.

"Well," Kelly continues, "have you made your choice?"

The woman smiles and nods her head yes. The crowd of people that has gathered around us cheers and claps. "Let's hear it!" they shout.

"That one," she says, pointing to the plate to my left. I make a big show of revealing the plate's identity. I twirl it around a few times in the air and then turn it over for everyone to see. Kelly is supposed to read it out loud, and she does, with a booming voice.

"The Olympic Diner!" she shouts.

I rush to the scoreboard and draw a line underneath the Olympic Diner heading. Some of the people in the crowd applaud. Others are laughing. I get the feeling they think we're just "cute kids." Usually, I hate that, but right now I don't care. I'll take all the support I can get, any way it comes.

Next up is a man who's wearing a white smock with red spots on it. He must be from the meat-packing plant. He quickly wolfs down both hamburger pieces. Right away he points to the hamburger he's chosen. I lift the plate and show the bottom of it to the crowd. They read it out for me. "The Olympic Diner!" More applause. I draw one more line on the Olympic Diner side of the scoreboard.

By this time it's the heart of the lunch rush. Bumper-to-bumper traffic clogs the street, as people head home or to the restaurants. Dozens of people are streaming out of the meat-packing plants and a lot of them come our way. There are so many people around our booth that they're crunched tightly into one another. But they seem to love it. It's getting hard for Kelly to shout over all the noise. I wish I had brought a megaphone.

Our next taste-tester is a big fat man with grey whiskers. His belly flops over his belt like a sack of potatoes. Everybody goes nuts when he walks up to the booth. They hoot and holler and egg him on.

"If anybody knows hamburgers," someone shouts, "it's Tiny!" The crowd howls with laughter.

Tiny eats the hamburger pieces slowly, taking small bites and chewing long. He's taking his sweet old time about it. Nobody says a word while he's chewing. It's totally silent. Kelly and I have begun to sweat from the hot midday sun. I take a peek over at Super Burger and my heart almost drops when I see the parking lot full of cars and people standing in long lines at the ordering counter. Over at the Olympic Diner there's hardly any business.

"Have you made a decision, sir?" Kelly asks Tiny.

Tiny gulps down his last swallow of the hamburger pieces. "Yes, I have," he says. He picks up the winning plate himself and holds it high above his head. Then he waves his arms across his face with the plate up high so everybody in the crowd can see the name of the restaurant written on the bottom. I'm dying to see which restaurant he's chosen, but he's holding the writing away from Kelly and me.

"The Olympic Diner," someone in the crowd reads out.

I walk over to the scoreboard, proud as can be, and mark one more line on the Olympic Diner's side. Just like I'd hoped, everyone's choosing the Olympic Diner hamburger over Super Burger's.

As soon as Tiny's choice is revealed to the crowd, a man yells out, "So what are we all doing here? Lunch at the Olympic Diner! Let's go!"

Sure enough, he and his friends head towards the Olympic Diner, with Tiny trailing after them. They stream through the front door, one after another. I wish I could be there to see Uncle Nick's face right now, as the new customers walk in. He must be surprised. And super happy.

The crowd around us has thinned out a bit because lunch is almost over, but we still have at least fifteen people at our booth. Roger from our team has shown up, and we ask him to go buy more hamburgers for us because we're running out. Kelly and I continue the Great Burger Taste-Off. The score is now Olympic Diner 18, Super Burger 2.

Then it happens. Kelly and I don't notice right away because we're busy serving people burgers and pop for the taste test. But we hear the crowd shuffling frantically so we lift our heads to see what's going on.

There's a white van parked on the boulevard about thirty metres away from us. A ramp spills out of the van onto the boulevard. Two men come out of the van, rolling an enormous TV camera in front of them. I look closer at the van and notice a bright red TV 5 insignia painted on the side. I guess Kelly's mom came through for us.

The men with the camera are headed right for us. The crowd is full of excitement, and everybody's head is turned. Finally the men with the camera crush their way through the crowd and set up the camera right in front of the Great Burger Taste-Off booth. Then another man, wearing a suit and tie and with perfect brown hair, walks out of the van.

"I've seen that guy on TV," someone exclaims. The crowd ogles the man as he strolls up to us.

"Hugh McMaster, kids," the man says. "From TV 5 News. Nice to meet you."

Kelly and I shake his hand. The taste test is temporarily stopped, but more of a crowd than ever has suddenly gathered.

"I hear you kids are up to something very interesting here today," the news man says. "Which one of you would like to tell me what exactly's going on?"

Kelly and I look at one another kind of funny, and then I speak. "As you can see from the banner," I start, surprising myself at how confident I am, "we're holding a Great Burger Taste-Off. We're asking people to choose between Super Burger's and the Olympic Diner's hamburgers."

"Looks like a lot of people are interested," the news man says, nodding towards the crowd.

"Does look that way, doesn't it?" Kelly laughs.

"Well, kids, I don't want you to be scared. What we want to do is a short feature for tonight's six o'clock news on you two and The First Annual Great Burger Taste-Off. Just go about everything as you were before we got here. The camera guys'll shoot some footage, and then I'll ask you both a few questions. On camera, of course. It won't hurt a bit. In fact, it's a lot easier than going to the dentist's."

Kelly and I laugh, but nervously because now we're scared. We didn't really expect the Great Burger Taste-Off to get *this* big. I've never been on TV before. All of a sudden I start worrying about how I look. So does everybody in the crowd. They start acting funny, weird.

But we go on with the Taste-Off anyhow, and the Olympic Diner continues steamrolling over Super Burger. The score's now Olympic Diner 27, Super Burger 5. After a while I forget the camera's pointed at us, even though it is hard to ignore the red flashing light on the camera's side. Hugh McMaster asks Kelly and me some questions. We try our best to answer smartly. I tell Hugh McMaster why I'm holding the Taste-Off, how I got the idea, and he seems genuinely interested. I also keep glancing over at the Olympic Diner and see a whole lot of people going in and coming out. The Taste-Off has been great for business.

Before long, the news crew is all done and they return to their van and drive off. Kelly and I have run out of hamburgers by then. The scoreboard tells the story: Olympic Diner 34, Super Burger 6. The crowd around us is down to only a few of the kids from the neighbourhood hanging around on their bikes. Everyone else has gone home or back to work. Kelly and I clean up and pack our things together. We take everything — the booth, the scoreboard, the sign — back to Kelly's garage. Kelly wants to call her mom and tell her about what's happened. I tell her I'm going to check on Uncle Nick. We shake hands.

"That was sure a lot of fun," Kelly says. "Thanks for asking me to help."

"Thanks for helping," I say. "I couldn't have done it without you." I smile and lay my hands out to trade skin with her. Kelly gets right into it the way I taught her.

"See you."

"See you."

I don't know whether Kelly is my girlfriend or not. And I don't care. All I know is she's my *best* friend.

When I finally get back to the Olympic Diner about an hour later, I can tell right away that the place has been a lot busier than usual. There are dirty dishes piled up a dozen high in several rows behind the counter. The chairs and the tables have been turned every which way. The garbage pails are spilling over. And what a sight Vera and Uncle Nick are! Vera looks totally pooped. As for Uncle Nick, he's sitting down in a chair in the kitchen, his legs spread out wide, his shoulders pushed far back. A damp cloth is spread over his forehead.

"Where were you, kiddo?" Vera asks me. "Could we ever have used your help today!"

"It was really something," Uncle Nick says, sitting up and wiping his face with the damp cloth.

"I'll help you clean up," I say.

"Clean up?" Uncle Nick says. "No way! Not for a little while at least."

Then Uncle Nick continues: "Why clean up so fast? I want to sit back and look at the diner like this. It's beautiful. I love it. I had so much fun today, Tommy, making hamburgers for everybody, hurrying to keep up with the orders. It was almost like old times."

# 14

## Stars of the Six O'Clock News

I keep my mouth shut. Part of me wants to tell Uncle Nick and Vera all about the Great Burger Taste-Off, but another part of me, the stronger part, wants to wait until the TV 5 news to surprise them.

We start cleaning the Olympic Diner, and I really hustle to keep up with Uncle Nick and Vera. They're sure hard workers. Uncle Nick is scouring all the cooking equipment with pads of steel wool, while Vera scrubs all the counters with soap and water. I mop the front floor and tidy up the tables and chairs. I also keep wondering whether the Olympic Diner will stay busy now or whether everybody will just go back tomorrow to eating at Super Burger.

When it's just about six o'clock, I ask Uncle Nick if I can bring his TV into the diner. He looks puzzled, but I tell him it's important. I set the TV up next to the cash register, with the screen facing the kitchen where we can all see it. I turn the dial to Channel 5. I don't think I've ever been this excited before in my life. Not even for a baseball game. My body feels like it wants to jump out of my skin.

A newscaster comes on and reads the news. It's not Hugh McMaster but an older man with white hair. I keep waiting to see the Great Burger Taste-Off, but the white-haired newscaster drones on and on about everything but. I'm getting anxious. I'm actually shaking as I mop the floor. Uncle Nick and Vera go about their cleaning without paying much attention to the TV.

Finally, the news is broken by a bunch of commercials, and I move up to the set and turn up the volume. Hugh McMaster must be next, I think. But I'm wrong. The weather man comes out in front of a wall-length map of Canada and chalks out the temperatures across the country. When I see Toronto I get this funny feeling like I miss it and I don't, both at the same time. Then there's more commercials, and then a woman comes out to read the sports scores. I'm beginning to think something has gone wrong. Maybe Hugh McMaster decided against doing a feature on the Great Burger Taste-Off. Maybe he found something better to report on.

And then the woman sportscaster swivels in her chair and says, "That's all for sports. When we come back, newscaster Hugh McMaster will present a fascinating story of two youngsters in search of the perfect hamburger."

My stomach feels like the inside of a pinball machine. *Poink! Clang! Bang!* I feel like I'm running in a thousand different directions at once, only I'm actually standing still in one spot. I think of calling Kelly, but just then the phone rings. I race to answer it before anybody else does, and sure enough it's Kelly, as excited as I am.

"Did you see that? We're next!"

"I can't wait, Kelly. This is almost painful."

"I hope they make us look good."

"So do I."

"The commercial's ending. Talk to you later."

"Later."

I turn the volume on the TV even higher. Uncle Nick and Vera perk up their heads, like they're annoyed. Vera starts to say "Turn it down," but I interrupt her.

"Sit down," I say. "You'll want to watch this."

The news feature begins with a closeup of a boxing ring and a bell tolling like the beginning of a boxing match. Then the words "Battle of the Burgers" appears on the screen, over the ring. Then there's a shot of Hugh McMaster on the Frontenac Street boulevard, with the Great Burger Taste-Off booth in the background. You can hear the traffic passing and you can see the crowd of people that had gathered around the booth.

Hugh McMaster explains the Taste-Off, exactly the way I explained it to him. He calls the Olympic Diner "one of Winnipeg's secret treasures, a time capsule back to an era when Fats Domino was on the jukebox and real beef was on the grill." Then there's a closeup of one of the taste-testers chomping on the two pieces of hamburger. When he's done, Hugh McMaster pulls him aside to talk with him, and he says how it's great these kids have come up with such an original idea.

Then you see Kelly and me talking with Hugh McMaster. We tell him we're doing this for my uncle, because we know he has the best-tasting hamburgers in the neighbourhood. We tell about how everybody seems to have suddenly forgotten the Olympic Diner since Super Burger moved into town, but we hope the Great Burger Taste-Off will change all that.

Hugh McMaster turns away from me then and looks straight into the camera and says a bunch of nice things about me. He calls me "a young man with a wonderful imagination and an admirable sense of family loyalty." He makes me sound like some sort of hero.

Then the camera zooms in on Hugh McMaster's face. He brings a hamburger up to his mouth and I can tell right away it's from the Olympic Diner because it's big and fat and juicy. He munches that hamburger like it's the best he's ever tasted. Then the camera sweeps around, passing Super Burger's bright blue sign and stopping on the gold and orange Olympic Diner sign. You can hear Hugh McMaster saying, "From Frontenac Street in Windsor Park, Winnipeg, this is Hugh McMaster."

And then it's over.

Vera rushes over to me and squeezes me hard. There are actually tears in her eyes. "That was so beautiful, kiddo. So beautiful."

Uncle Nick suddenly bursts out laughing. Loud, crazy laughter that comes out of his chest in waves. All through the time the feature was being shown on TV he had been silent, kind of amazed, so caught by surprise, I guess, that he couldn't say anything. Now he's roaring with laughter and clapping his hands. He looks like a man who's just struck gold.

"No wonder we were so busy today," Uncle Nick says finally. "Tommy, the best thing you ever did was come up here this summer. I think you've just saved the Olympic Diner, something your uncle couldn't do himself."

He moves to me then and gives me a big hug, and I hug him back. He starts dancing the way I've seen my mom's friends dance at Greek parties. His arms are flung out from his sides, and he's snapping his fingers. He twirls around in tight circles and every so often bounds high into the air and taps his heel with his right hand, shouting "Opa!" just as his fingers rap his shoe.

Then Uncle Nick reaches out for me and I join him. We weave our arms together and continue his Greek dance. Which is weird, because I've always thought Greek dancing was silly. I mean, my mom's tried a thousand times to get me up to dance with her and her friends and I always just run away. And now Uncle Nick just reaches out for me and there I am twirling and kicking with him and letting loose in the dance, feeling it's a cool way of celebrating, like a running back doing some fancy steps in the end zone after scoring a touchdown.

I can't believe it. We won our last game and I played well. And now I've helped save the Olympic Diner. Things looked so awful to me just a few days ago. Now things look so good I don't think I ever want to leave Winnipeg. All of a sudden I feel like the Windsor Park Red Sox can beat the West Side Giants and win the Little League baseball championship. I feel important. Like people need me.

But there's no time to sit and feel good. No way. Just as soon as Uncle Nick shuts off the TV the phone starts ringing and people start dropping by. Everybody wants to talk to Uncle Nick about the TV feature. Everybody wants to meet me. And everybody wants to try an Olympic Diner hamburger.

Before long all the revolving stools at the counter are taken, and so are most of the tables. I guess word about our TV appearance has even spread to the meat-packing plants, because a lot of the late shifters come in for their dinner break. People are talking loud and having fun. Everybody's in a good mood.

Uncle Nick slaps hamburger patties onto the barbecue without even looking, and they fall in neat lines.

Meanwhile, I hurry to dress the buns with mustard, relish, onions and Uncle Nick's chili sauce. Vera takes everybody's order and hands them their plates. We're an unbeatable team, like a shortstop, second baseman and first baseman working countless double plays. I'm on top of the world.

# 15

## The Playoff

Already during my summer vacation, I've gone from feeling mad to depressed to guilty to excited to happy. I guess I should have known there had to be something after happy.

That something comes at our next game. We're playing the Forest Park Cardinals, at Forest Park. It's the playoff, and the winner will meet the West Side Giants in the twelve-year-old Little League championship game.

Before the game, I sit in the Olympic Diner and Uncle Nick makes me an Olympic Diner Platter. I gobble it up eagerly and chat with Uncle Nick. He tells me he's going to try to make the game, but if the diner is busy, it'll be hard for him to get away.

Business has really picked up at the diner, thanks to the Great Burger Taste-Off. Uncle Nick and I are really getting along well. I try to teach him as much as I can about baseball, and he shows me all he can about how things work at the diner. And Kelly and I have been going swimming, playing catch, and doing a whole lot of things together. We've even had lunch together a few times at Uncle Nick's.

Gord Yamoto's dad is supposed to drive us to Forest Park. Kelly and I meet Gord and Glen Arnason at the Windsor Park clubhouse. We pile into Gord's father's car and head for Forest Park. The guys tell Kelly and me how cool we looked on TV. They want to know all about the Great Burger Taste-Off. Everybody in the car's hyped. We know we can beat the Cardinals. And we can't wait to get our hands on the Giants.

I'm thinking a little about what'll happen if Jeff pitches today and he has to throw a curve ball, but the thought doesn't worry me too much. Somehow I believe that now I'm ready to handle even Jeff's curve ball.

We make up a rap song about our team there in the back seat of the car. Glen's real good at rhyming and comes up with neat lines like, "The Red Sox you cannot beat, we are mean, angry and fast on our feet." Gord adds the back beat, loudly spitting out an endless series of "Pa-too, pa-too, pa-too's."

I sing along and look out the window at the strange city. It's a lot different than Toronto. It doesn't look like it's hurrying to get anywhere. We cross a bridge now that spreads over a wide, muddy river. The bridge dips and then comes back up again and at the very top of the rise you can see the downtown area like it's right there in front of you, the tall buildings looming like the turrets of a giant castle.

All of us are having so much fun nobody notices Gord's dad is lost until he stops the car and pulls a city map out of the glove compartment. He's looking at it carefully. I can tell he's confused.

"Do any of you know how to get to Forest Park?" he asks us finally.

"Dad, you've got to be kidding! The game starts in fifteen minutes." Gord cries out.

"I wish I were kidding, Gord. I know the park's somewhere around here, but there are so many bays and dead-ends in this neighbourhood I just can't seem to get there."

"Isn't it on Mosienko Drive?" Kelly says.

"That's right, it is," Gord's dad says, "but how do we get to Mosienko Drive?"

"Beats me," Kelly says.

"We're going to miss infield practice," Glen says.

"Let's hope we don't miss the start of the game," Gord's dad says.

"No way!" Gord pouts.

My stomach starts up again. I thought I was through with butterflies, but they're down there again, fluttering around. What if we miss the game? What if the Red Sox have to forfeit because we don't show up? Then we'd miss out on our chance to win the championship.

Gord's dad drives to a gas station and runs in to ask directions, but we're already way too late. Even if we make it there in five minutes, we'll have to take the field right away. I won't have a chance to warm up the pitcher. I won't even have a chance to warm myself up.

Gord's dad returns and shifts the car into gear. We rocket out of the gas station and back onto the street. He takes two turns and just like that we're on Mosienko Drive. Gord's dad takes a deep breath. We all crane our necks looking for the ballpark. We spot it about five blocks down.

Gord's dad slips his car next to where Coach's truck is parked. The second the car makes a full stop, the guys dart out like rescue workers out of an ambulance. All four of us run out to the diamond as fast as we can.

Lucky for us, the game hasn't started yet. I can see all the Cardinals players gathered in a circle around their coach. That means they're about to take their at-bat and our pitcher must still be warming up. My stomach settles down. I look over at the pitching mound and see Jeff there. I figure Coach Minuk must be warming him up, waiting for me. Gord, Glen and

Kelly run straight out to the field while I head for the duffel bag in the dugout to dig out my batcatcher's equipment.

But it's not there.

I tool inside the bag, but can't find a thing. Not the mask, not the chest protector, not the shin guards. I'm going crazy. What's happening here? Is this somebody's idea of a practical joke? Maybe Jeff's? Finally, I turn the bag upside down and let everything fall out. Bats and balls drop to the ground. But no catcher's equipment.

I decide to run out to Coach and find out what's going on. I bolt madly for home plate. And then I stop dead in my tracks.

Coach isn't at home plate. He's over by first base talking to the infield umpire. There's a guy I don't think I've ever seen before behind home plate, warming up Jeff. He's wearing all the catcher's equipment, including the mask, so I can't see his face. I just can't understand what's going on. This catcher can't be a new guy, because the cut-off date for new players was the last game of the regular season. Then who is he? Just then the catcher takes off his mask. I have no idea who he is. He's good-looking, with blond hair and blue eyes. He's about five centimetres taller than me and his shoulders are wide over his chest. He moves up to me and puts out his hand. I shake it.

"You're Tom Poulos, right?" he says.

"Yes."

"My name's Frank Mitchell. I'm the regular batcatcher. Coach said I start today."

The words hit me like a brick wall I've just run into. Frank trots back behind the plate.

Jeff shouts at me from the pitching mound. "You can go home, T.O. We've got a real catcher here now." There's a nasty smile pasted on his face.

"Play ball!" the umpire yells.

I get off the diamond fast. I look out at the players and know I belong there with them. I helped them make it this far. I helped them win our last game against the Giants.

I take a seat on the bench next to Roger Frechette. "Don't hold it against Frank," he says. "His dad was called back to work so his family had to cut their holiday short. He made it back into town last night."

I don't say anything.

"Look on the bright side," Roger says. "You don't have to catch for Jeff."

I still don't say anything. I can't believe this is happening to me.

Coach trots back to the dugout then and sits beside me.

"I'm sorry, Tom," he says, "I had to start Frank today. He works well with Jeff. He can catch Jeff's curve and we might have to use it tonight if the game's close."

"I understand," I say. But I don't. Not really.

"You're a real good catcher," Coach continues. "In fact, I don't think we'd be here today if you hadn't helped us out. But I had to go with the man I felt could do the best job in this particular situation. Hang in there. I may need you yet."

I don't believe him. His starting catcher's back now and he's going to go with him. Any coach who wanted to win would do exactly the same.

I look at my Ernie Whitt mitt and feel like pulling it off my hand and hurling it against the dugout fence. What good is it to me now?

But I stop myself. I think of what Uncle Nick told me after my first game, when I was such a sore loser. *You can't worry about the things you can't control.* Frank Mitchell's back, and Coach has decided to start him. I can't do anything about that. So I won't try. And I won't worry about it. But if Coach Minuk does need me, I'll be ready. I'm going to show everyone that I'm a real batcatcher.

Minuk does need me, I'll be ready. I'm going to show everyone that I'm a real batcatcher.

In the meantime, I remind myself, that's my team out there on the diamond, playing in a very important game. One thing I can do is cheer them on. Whether I'm behind the plate or not right now, I'm part of this team and I want them to win. I get up off that bench and start hollering at the guys. "You can do it!" and "Go Red Sox!" Kelly's nearby over on third base and she waves back at me.

Jeff's mixing up his pitches, confusing the Cardinals batters. They're not connecting at all. They're a smaller team than the Giants. Our guys look loose out there, like they know they can win this game.

I fix my eyes on Frank Mitchell. He's the kind of catcher you'd be scared to steal second base on because he looks so confident behind the plate. He catches Jeff's pitches without too much difficulty, even some wild throws that veer high and outside.

I'd be lying if I said part of me isn't hoping Frank Mitchell will do something stupid. Drop a pitch. Flub a foul pop-up. Louse up a throw. Part of me wants him to look bad. Not so bad that the team will lose as a result, but bad enough so Coach and the guys can see that I deserve to be the team's batcatcher.

I know I should be rooting for the team full-out, including Frank Mitchell. But I can't. I don't know if this makes me a bad person. But I'm trying not to feel this way, trying to make myself want to see Frank Mitchell play well. That's good, isn't it?

The game moves along fast, mostly because Jeff does away with the Cardinals batters like they're so many cardboard ducks at a shooting gallery. One after the other they go down. They strike out, they pop up, they squiggle hits into the eager hands of our infield.

Our guys do a lot better against the Cardinals pitcher, but we don't score too many runs either. All our hits come scattered. By the end of five innings we're stuck with only two runs. But at least our two runs are two more than the Cardinals have mustered.

That's when Frank Mitchell comes by and sits down next to me on the bench.

"I appreciate you filling in for me last two games," he says.

"No problem," I say. I don't look him in the eyes. I just stare at the ground.

"Those West Side Giants sure are a tough team. Did they try hammering you whenever they crossed home plate?"

"I guess so. They play rough."

"I'm surprised we beat them. I hear you got some good hits."

"Yeah," I say. I turn up my head to face him. "I did all right."

I'm finding that I kind of like Frank Mitchell. I thought he'd be like Jeff and those two friends of his who banged up the pinball machine in the Olympic Diner. But he's not. He's a friendly, easygoing guy. I decide to tell him how much trouble I had with Jeff's curve ball. "But I kind of ruined things in the first game. Jeff started throwing his curve, and I just lost it then. There was no way I could catch it. My mitt was everywhere but in front of the ball."

"No way," Frank Mitchell says. "I've never had a problem with Jeff's curve. Maybe because I'm bigger than you or something."

"Maybe."

"I tell you, though, I've lost my batting swing. Three weeks with no practice and you get rusty."

It's true. So far today Frank's batting record is 0 for 3. As good as he's been behind the plate, he hasn't been able to so much as foul-tip the ball at the plate. I had felt kind of good earlier about him striking out, but now I feel kind of bad.

"You'll come around by next game," I say.

"Hope so," he says.

Then Mrs. Minuk calls out Frank's name because he's on deck. He scoots off the bench and grabs a bat and starts practice swinging. As I watch him, I'm hoping he manages a hit when he goes up to bat.

But he doesn't. He strikes out again. I can tell he's looking for a home run, when he should just be concentrating on laying wood on the ball.

When the last inning begins, Coach has a long chat at the pitcher's mound with Jeff and Frank. I figure he's telling Jeff to let loose with the curve ball as insurance against the Cardinals catching up. I stand up off the bench and pay closer attention to the game. I want to see this.

Sure enough, the curve ball it is. Jeff winds up like a spinning tornado and releases the ball with a lashing whip motion. The ball zooms to the plate then zips up and around the hitter's bat. And right into Frank Mitchell's catcher's mitt.

Jeff even dirty-looks me from the mound, like he's telling me, *See, a real catcher knows how to catch a curve ball.*

Same thing happens on the next pitch. Jeff unleashes a whipping curve, the batter swings way under the ball, and *Smack!* the ball pounds into Frank's mitt.

I can't believe this. I have to watch again, this time keeping my eyes focused on Frank Mitchell.

And then I see it. I see the secret to catching Jeff's curve ball. And it's not Frank being bigger than I am, and it's not Frank being quicker than I am. All it is is Frank setting himself farther away from the plate. By the time the ball reaches Frank, it's already broken into its new path. He has time to adjust his mitt to the ball's new direction. I can tell it's just something Frank does without even thinking about it. As he squats, he bounces a few centimetres back on the balls of his feet. That's it!

I know I can catch a curve ball now. I was rushing it, trying to predict the curve, and missing by a mile. All I have to do is wait out the pitch, see how it's breaking, and adjust my mitt to catch it.

I can't wait to try out my new knowledge. I wish Coach would put me in right now. But he doesn't, of course. Jeff's curve ball totally mixes up the Cardinals and they go down one-two-three. The game's over.

The guys all rush to the dugout and jump up and down together, lifting Jeff up onto their shoulders. We've made it to the championship game! I'm jumping along with everybody else. This is my team now. We have one game left. If we beat the West Side Giants we'll be the twelve-year-old Little League champions.

I didn't think I'd be this happy about the Windsor Park Red Sox making it to the championship, but I'm feeling the same way I felt last year when the Jarvis Badgers made it to the City of Toronto semi-finals. It's like I'm floating on air.

More than anything I want to play in that championship game. I know I can catch a curve ball now. I know I can. I want to play in that championship game so badly. I just have to. But somehow I know I won't.

# 16

# Uncle Nick Tries Pitching

Uncle Nick is waiting inside his car to pick me up. He honks so I can hear him. I rush out of the dugout and scoot into the passenger seat.

"How was the game?"

"Great." I say, truly excited. "We won."

"Way to go, Tommy. Did you do well?"

"I didn't get to play," I say. All of a sudden I feel a little sad.

Uncle Nick doesn't say a thing. I guess he's afraid I'll treat him mean the way I did after that first game, when we lost because I couldn't catch Jeff's curve balls. But I'm not going to do that. I'm not going to be a baby this time.

"Too bad you missed the game, Uncle Nick," I say. "It was a good one. Even though I didn't get to play."

There's hardly any traffic, and Uncle Nick manoeuvres the car through the streets with little effort. I'm reminded of that first drive we took back from the airport. I think of how much better I've gotten to know Uncle Nick since then, how much more he means to me now. I look at him now, and he looks at me, and his eyes seem to be saying that he's thinking the same thing I'm thinking, and we smile.

Uncle Nick fishes a dried fig from his pocket and holds it out to me. I take it and pop it into my mouth. It feels cool.

I guess Uncle Nick senses that even though I'm not whining about riding the bench today, I'd be a lot happier if I had been able to play. "Didn't go the way you wanted it today, did it?" he asks and flicks a fig into his mouth.

"Yes and no."

Uncle Nick laughs softly and shakes his head. "So many things seem to be yes and no at the same time, don't they?" he says.

"That's for sure. I mean, we won the game today and we're in the finals against the West Side Giants, and I'm really happy about that. But I didn't get to play. The real catcher is back from his holidays. I don't think I'll get to play in the championship game either. I don't like that one bit."

"I guess I can't blame you. You love to play. It would be a shame if you couldn't play."

We're driving over a bridge now, but it's another one, not the one that passes over the river. This bridge passes over a thick tangle of railroad tracks. I can see old boxcar trains down there that look like they haven't moved in a hundred years. The tracks run every which way, like a maze. Beside the tracks there's a huge building with rows of wooden doors across it.

"Your father and I used to unload crates from trains into that building down there," Uncle Nick says. "Heavy crates full of all sorts of things. They don't use that building anymore."

"My father lived here?" I ask. I didn't know that.

"Didn't your mother ever tell you? It was before you were born, right after we moved to Canada from Greece. The three of us — your mother, your father and I — lived together in an apartment over there." Uncle Nick points to some old apartment blocks next to a church with an onion top. "But your father and mother didn't stay long. They moved to Toronto after a year. They couldn't stand the cold here in the winter. They said Toronto's winters weren't so bad."

"Why'd you stay?"

"I was working at the Olympic Diner nights. My godfather owned it back then. He promised to sell it to me one day. I wanted to wait for that day. I loved the Olympic Diner from the time I first laid eyes on it."

"Didn't you ever miss Greece, Uncle Nick?" I ask. "You're always saying how beautiful it is."

"Sure I missed it, but I don't miss it anymore. For the longest time, I remember, I'd wake up in the middle of the night, sweating and breathing hard. I'd be dreaming about our village in Greece, about our house up on the rocky hill and the valley of fig and almond trees below it. I couldn't sleep because that picture was stuck in my mind, haunting me like a nightmare. Then, finally, a few years ago, I took a trip back. I saw it all again. A lot was the same as I had left it, a lot had changed. But I saw it, and after I saw it I knew for sure that as much as my home village meant to me, the Olympic Diner was where my hopes and dreams were. I've never had those nightmares again."

We keep driving, and the sun is red and round and sinking into the earth.

"I don't get it, Uncle Nick," I say then. "I had such a great game last week, and I had so much fun putting on the Great Burger Taste-Off, but now Frank Mitchell comes back to the team and they don't need me anymore. Just when things look like they're going to be OK, something happens to push me back."

"Something always happens," Uncle Nick says. "Something good, something bad, there's always *something* happening."

"What do you mean?"

"You can't count on what you want happening all the time. Sometimes it does, sometimes it doesn't. But you never know what to expect. There's always the chance something will come at you out of the blue. I guess all you can do is be as strong as you can be. Then whatever comes at you, you're ready."

"Sounds to me a lot like catching a curve ball."

Uncle Nick thinks that one over. His bushy eyebrows bunch together. "I guess it's a lot like that, Tommy."

I can tell we're almost home now by the strong smell of the meat-packing plants wafting through the windows. It's funny, but I don't mind that smell anymore.

"The best times of all, Tommy, are when you *make* something happen yourself. The way you made the Olympic Diner come alive again."

"I guess the Great Burger Taste-Off worked."

"That was something that happened to me," Uncle Nick says, "that I didn't expect. And it was the greatest thing that could ever have happened."

It's just beginning to get dark as we pull into the Olympic Diner parking lot.

"Look at that," Uncle Nick says, jokingly. "Vera hasn't even turned on the sign yet." He laughs. "How many times do I have to tell her to turn that sign on the second the sun starts setting."

We walk out of the car. Uncle Nick opens the door for me. There are quite a few customers at the counter.

"How's business been while I was gone?" Uncle Nick asks Vera.

"Not bad," Vera answers back. "But don't worry. I handled everything."

"No problems?"

"No problems."

Uncle Nick slips into the bathroom, where the circuit box is, to turn on the Olympic Diner sign. He comes back and sits and talks with the customers. I take off through the kitchen for the back room and pull off my uniform. It's too clean for my liking. I wish I'd been able to muck it up a bit. I put on my jeans and my Toronto Blue Jays T-shirt.

When I get back inside the Olympic Diner, Uncle Nick is waiting for me with a milkshake. He hasn't poured it into a wax cup, but left it inside the tin container. I like it better that way. I take a sip through the straw. Tastes great.

Uncle Nick is fiddling with that baseball he keeps with him all the time now. He's rubbing his hands over it and, from what I can figure, trying to get the proper curve ball grip around the seams. I can tell he'd like to play catch with me right now, help me practise. I don't know what to do. What use would a practice with Uncle Nick be? At the same time, though, I don't want to hurt his feelings again.

"Let's go outside and play catch," I say to him then. It's a crazy idea, but it's worth it if it'll make Uncle Nick happy. "It'll be fun."

"No, I'm not good enough to help you, Tommy," Uncle Nick says.

"Any practice at all will help," I say. I owe him.

Uncle Nick tosses the ball up into the air with a flick of his wrist and catches it eagerly with both his hands. "OK," he says, smiling. "Let's give this a try."

I finish my milkshake and go back to my room to get my catcher's mitt.

"Meet you in the parking lot," Uncle Nick calls out to me.

Once we're outside in the Olympic Diner parking lot, Uncle Nick starts loosening up, rolling his shoulders, stretching his arms.

I'm holding the baseball and my catcher's mitt. Uncle Nick is wearing a shirt with a design of colourful flowers on it and dress pants and his fancy black shoes.

"I think I can do this," Uncle Nick says, studying the baseball in his hand as if he's looking for some sort of clue about how to throw it. "Maybe your mother never told you, Tommy," he continues, "but our family owned a whole flock of sheep — sixty-seven we had one year — when we lived in Greece. We'd go up into the mountains over our village to let the sheep graze and it was my job, when I was about your age, to make sure none of the sheep got lost or left the flock. If I'd see one roaming too far away, I'd have to take a rock and throw it at a spot right in front of them so they'd get scared and come back to the flock. I had great aim. I could throw a rock at a target halfway up the mountain."

I'm not exactly sure if that particular skill will come in handy when Uncle Nick tries to throw a baseball, but I decide to keep the thought to myself. The last thing I want to do is make him feel bad again.

"I think the best thing for us to do, Uncle Nick, is to have you pitch to me," I say. "I'll get down into my catcher's stance over here and you can pitch to me from about twelve metres away. If any balls get past me, they'll just rebound off the building." I point to the far side of the Olympic Diner, which is directly behind me right now.

"Sounds fine with me," Uncle Nick says. "I'm dying to try my curve ball out."

I know Uncle Nick won't be able to throw a curve ball, but I decide the practice will be good for me anyhow. I take an aluminum garbage can cover and place it in front of me to serve as home plate.

Uncle Nick pats me on the back and starts walking away from me with huge steps the way you do when you're counting out a first down in football. When he's the proper distance away, he calls out, "Ready, Tommy."

I'm kind of nervous, not for myself, but for Uncle Nick. I want him to be good enough to be able to practise with me. I really do. I don't want him to feel bad. I fling the ball then to Uncle Nick, not too hard but hard enough because he's pretty far away from me. He nabs it out of the air in his bare right hand and the ball hitting the skin of his palm makes a smacking sound in the quiet evening air. Uncle Nick doesn't so much as flinch. I guess his hands are too tough from all that work he does in the diner to sting easily. He rubs the ball with his hands. I crouch down into my squat.

"Ready," I say. "Start with some normal throws until we're warmed up."

Uncle Nick nods his head. He doesn't look like much of a pitcher in those fancy clothes of his, but he's trying his best.

"OK, Tommy, here comes."

Uncle Nick starts his windup. I can tell he's studying his every move, like he's trying to learn a new dance step. His left leg rises, then lunges forward. His right arm is cocked at the side of his head.

So far, so good.

Then everything goes wrong. I guess he's never thrown a baseball before, because he loses his grip and the ball goes flying wildly a metre over my head. I bounce up to trap it in my mitt, but there's no way. The ball bounces off the Olympic Diner wall.

But Uncle Nick's not fazed. He runs out to the ball, the heels of his shoes clicking against the pavement. He picks the ball up and hustles back to his pitching spot.

"Let's try that again," he says and laughs. "Your mother could've thrown better than that."

"Don't push so much," I suggest. "Just kind of throw the ball."

"You're right," he says. "I know what I did wrong."

Uncle Nick winds up again, just as carefully as the first time. This time, though, he keeps his right hand tighter around the ball, and his arm doesn't push out from the elbow, but actually whips the ball out of his hand.

I'm amazed. The ball comes whizzing straight at me, way faster than I'd expected. It's a strike, too, headed right for the pocket of my mitt. I can't believe it. The ball bangs into my mitt, stinging my hand. Uncle Nick sure got a lot of speed behind that one.

I figure this must be beginner's luck and toss the ball back to Uncle Nick. He catches it just as easily as before. I must say, he's a natural at catching a ball.

And then he winds up in that text book delivery of his and throws another perfect strike. And then another. And then another.

Maybe throwing rocks to scare stray sheep isn't a bad starting-off point for a pitcher after all, I think to myself.

I start moving my mitt around, holding up different targets. Uncle Nick doesn't make each target, but he's always close, and he hasn't cut down on his speed. I figure he must be throwing at least twice as fast as Jeff. I'm working hard to catch his pitches, making sure none of them gets away from me.

"Not bad, hey?" Uncle Nick calls out to me. He's grinning. The light from the Olympic Diner sign is glinting off his shoes. A circle of sweat has formed under the armpits of his dress shirt. "I really like this."

"Not bad? Great's more like it," I say back.

"Most of those were strikes, I think," Uncle Nick says, showing off his new baseball knowledge. "Wouldn't you say so, Tommy?"

I chuckle.

"I'm going to try some curve balls now," Uncle Nick says then.

"Throw away," I say.

I sit crouched and wait. I know the odds are against Uncle Nick throwing a curve ball, but I'm ready just in case. Anyhow, I figure, the practice can't hurt me.

Uncle Nick snakes the fingers of his right hand around the ball. He stares at my mitt, then starts into his windup. He does everything right. He twists his wrist as he releases the ball. He follows through. He aims just a little to the right of my mitt so the ball will curve back into it.

But the ball doesn't curve. Not a centimetre. It's a fast pitch that travels straight as an arrow right smack into my mitt.

"Let me try again," Uncle Nick says.

Again he winds up, and again he throws me a perfect fastball. But the pitch is as flat as a glass of pop left out of the fridge too long.

And again and again and again.

But no curve ball.

Uncle Nick's sweating even more now. He wipes his forehead with the sleeve of his left arm and pulls at his moustache. "This time," he says. "This time."

He unleashes another pitch, faster than anything I've ever had to catch before. I nab it with my mitt.

Uncle Nick holds his hands up at his sides. His head is leaning over, his eyes popping out.

"That one curved, didn't it? I think it curved."

"No, Uncle Nick. I don't think so."

"No, Tommy, I think it did. Just a bit."

"No, I don't think so."

"Are you sure?"

"Yeah, I'm sure."

"Well, you must be right," he says, chuckling. "You know better than me what a curve ball's supposed to look like."

Uncle Nick keeps trying to throw that curve ball until it gets too dark to see the ball anymore. He shakes his head every time he misses and slaps himself on the forehead. But he does it in a way that I know he's not too serious, that he just wants to make me laugh.

Finally, we decide to call it quits for the night. I don't mind too much that Uncle Nick hasn't been able to throw a curve ball. Sure, it would have been nice to see if I can catch one now, but it's been a pretty good practice anyhow.

I know I'm ready for the championship game now. Whether I play or not.

# 17

# The Big Game

Just by glancing around the West Side Giants ballpark, you know right away the twelve-year-old Little League championship is a Big Game.

Cars pack the parking lot and the side streets. There's not a single empty seat in the stands people are squished together so tightly. I spot Uncle Nick in that mess of people and wave to him. Some people have even brought their own lawn chairs and set them up behind the third base line. Out there, too, you can see a lot of kids sitting on their bicycles, just taking in the action, sucking on the straws of slurpees.

The West Side Giants against the Windsor Park Red Sox. This is it.

While the Giants take their infield practice, our guys play catch. I pair up with Kelly. The early afternoon sun blazes hot in our eyes. The whole team's stiff and nervous because so many people are watching. And the kind of watching they're doing today is different than usual. A lot of people here aren't the mothers, fathers, brothers or sisters of the guys out on the field. They're just fans, out to see some baseball. Some good baseball. We have to deliver the goods. Coach Minuk is a little nervous today, too. I can tell. He's dressed better than usual, wearing a brand new sweatsuit. He does a lot of talking with the umpires and the opposing coach. And by the way they move their hands and nod their heads, you know what they're talking about is serious.

Even though I'm going to be sitting on the bench, I'm excited about this game. I hold the scorecard in front of me with all the names of the Giants players on it and study their moves closely.

Our guys take the field and Jeff starts warming up. In a lot of ways the game's in his hands. In his right hand actually, the pitching one. He's got to come through for us today, and he knows it, and on that mound right now he's trying hard to work into his groove.

Roger Frechette takes a seat on the bench next to me. He doesn't look too bothered that he's not pitching right now.

"How's it going, Tom?"

"Great. Hope we can do it."

"Hope so too."

Coach returns to the bench then and takes a swig of water from the thermos. Mrs. Minuk gives him the crossed fingers signal. "Thanks," he says, "we can use some good luck. Today more than ever."

Just then the umpire calls out, "Play ball!"

Their first batter up's Kevin Kotyluk, a short guy who Roger says is the fastest guy in the league. I remember him as one of the guys who stole on me in the last game against the Giants.

Jeff starts his windup. Everybody — the fans, the players, the coaches — holds their breath, waiting.

That first pitch breaks the ice. It's a blistering fastball that streaks straight into Frank Mitchell's mitt.

The umpire shouts "Stee-rike!"

All of a sudden the game's for real, not something you're thinking too much about, waiting to happen, sweating over, but something happening right now.

Jeff tries a slider next. Soon as he's released the ball, Kotyluk crouches into a bunt stance. He holds the bat loosely in his hands so the bat absorbs the ball and the ball doesn't bounce too far. He takes off for first immediately. Frank runs for the ball and picks it up out of the basepath dirt. He whips it to Merv on first. But Kotyluk's too fast. He beats the throw by a split second.

Just then the Giants fans and players start up. Loud.

"Attaboy!"

"Way to go!"

"Let's see a steal!"

After a quick out, Brad Johnson is up. He's a big guy with muscles rippling out of his uniform sleeves. He stalks up to the plate and wags the bat around as if it's a toothpick, then tags the first pitch through first and second. Meanwhile, Kotyluk the speedster blazes all the way to third.

The clean-up hitter's the same guy who batted clean-up for the Giants in our last two games against them. Brad Johnson might have been big, but this guy — Joe Stemkowski — is bigger. He could walk down a high school hallway and nobody'd so much as cough the wrong way.

The outfielders fan out farther and Kelly steps back a bit in case Stemkowski drives a beeliner right at her. Our guys on the bench, myself included, stand up and grip the wire mesh of the dugout fence. This is something you want to see as close up as possible.

Jeff stalls almost a half minute on the mound. He keeps rubbing the ball and kicking his right shoe into the black dirt. Stemkowski stands tall at the plate.

When the pitch comes I know right away it's a curve ball. I've studied Jeff throwing those things so much I can tell one the second he releases the ball. Stemkowski swings at it, but misses by a mile, losing his balance. Frank dips back onto the heels of his feet and nabs the ball. Both runners stay put.

The Giants coach is barking away at the sidelines. His face is purple already.

"Don't worry about it. Just hit away!"

Stemkowski hits away all right. Far away! Jeff serves him up a fastball on a silver platter, and he socks it way over the outfielder's gloves. The ball sails through the blue sky and bounces off the hood of a car parked on the street. You can hear the whack of ball hitting metal all the way in our dugout.

Giants 3, Red Sox 0. All in the wink of an eye.

The Giants fans go wild, hooting and hollering so loud I can hardly hear the umpire shout "Batter up, please."

Frank, who's been talking with Jeff, hustles back behind the plate. Jeff keeps his eyes on the ground. If he lets this homer bother him, we can kiss the game goodbye.

He doesn't. One thing about Jeff, he never gives up. He comes back now with a deadly mix of fastballs and curve balls that strike out the next two Giants batters.

Mrs. Minuk finishes up some work on the scorecard on the clipboard in front of her and calls out the names of the first three batters. Coach moves through the dugout, patting some guys on the back, whispering things to others. The subs pour water from the thermos into plastic cups. We're a real team.

Glen sidles up to the plate. The Giants pitcher, Wes Weschuk, tugs at the bill of his cap and rears back for the pitch. His left arm almost scrapes the ground. Then he brings it around fast and hard, like a lion tamer's whip lashing against the ground. The ball burns a path to home plate. Glen lays his bat out for the bunt. He connects.

The pitch is so fast the ball bounces hard off Glen's bat. Hard and high and right into Weschuk's glove.

Frank's up now. He's been having trouble connecting, and you can see him fidgeting at the plate. His practice swings are jerky. I'm hoping he can get a hit and start something off.

First pitch is a change-up. Frank's fooled and swings ahead of the ball.

The guys on our bench are standing. We're rooting him on at the top of our lungs.

"You can do it, Frank."

"Let her rip."

"Do it!"

Frank digs in his cleats and takes some big, loopy practice swings. The Giants are razzing him, giving him a rough time. The pitch comes and it's an obvious ball.

High and outside. Frank goes chasing after it.

Strike two.

Next, Weschuk fires a curve ball. I sure am an expert at identifying those now. The ball breaks just before it reaches the plate. Frank cuts under it. No wood. The ball pounds into the catcher's mitt.

"You're out!" the umpire yells.

Frank walks back to the dugout, his bat trailing behind.

Kelly's up now. The outfielders adjust their positions, stepping back a few metres. If Kelly does connect, they don't want it to be for an extra-base hit.

First pitch, Weschuk tries a curve ball. Kelly's more than ready. She steps into the ball and catches it before it breaks. The ball goes hurtling over the shortstop's head, and Kelly races for first. The centrefielder hurries to the ball and wings it into the second baseman. Kelly holds on second.

Now it's our turn to go wild. You'd think Kelly had just hit a game-winning grand-slam homer the way our players and fans start howling. I see Uncle Nick up in the stands whistling loud as he can, with two fingers in his mouth.

Everybody's tense in the dugout, hoping that Jeff can bring Kelly home for our first run. We all know we have to start chipping away at that three-run lead soon as possible.

Jeff's there for us, as usual. He jumps on Weschuk's first pitch and bangs a line drive far into the outfield. The ball whizzes through the grass like a squirrel racing up a tree. Kelly dashes home, and Jeff slides into second base. Safe.

Jeff pats the dust off his pants and shirt while Gord walks up to the plate. Everybody in the dugout's slapping Kelly on the back for scoring our first run. I high-five with her. Mitch and Merv have climbed up on the bench and are rooting Gord on.

But Gord swings too soon on a Weschuk change-up and pops up to the shortstop. We're down 3 to 1 after one inning.

Coach holds everyone back a minute in the dugout before the guys hit the field for the second inning.

"Come on, guys. We've come this far, now let's go all the way. Jeff, keep mixing your pitches. Curve balls, fast balls, change-ups. You have to use everything you've got to get these guys out. There's no holding back. We can't let them open up that lead. It's going to be tough enough catching up from two runs down."

Jeff takes the matter into his own hands. As much as I don't like the guy, I'm admitting more and more that he's the best pitcher I've ever played with. He's humming pitches by the Giants batters like they're wearing blindfolds.

Three up. Three down.

All of us on the bench rush out to greet the players as they run to the dugout for our at-bats. My heart's pumping fast with excitement.

Miles, leading off the inning, crowds the plate and manages to get cuffed on the shoulder by one of Weschuk's pitches. He drops to the ground, his right hand hugging his left shoulder. Coach runs out to take a look at him.

"Bean ball!" we yell. "Throw out the pitcher."

"He was asking for it!" the Giants yell back.

After all the fuss dies down, Miles takes his base. And wouldn't you know it, he starts giving the pitcher a hard time from there too, taking a big lead and forcing Weschuk to keep an eye on him. Weschuk tries to pick Miles off a few times, but Miles just slides back safely each time. You can tell Miles is bugging Weschuk now like a mosquito down his shirt.

Weschuk loses it. His control goes haywire, and his pitches go wild. He walks Mitch and then he walks Merv. He's lucky Glen's a little too eager at the plate and strikes out on three guaranteed balls.

Now it's Frank's turn to take a crack at Weschuk. He has to produce right now.

Weschuk pitches him a fastball. Frank swings and misses. The guys on the bases are crying for help. Just one tap and someone can make it home.

Another fastball. Another miss.

Coach's hands are in fists at his side, and he's shaking them fast, his arms bent at the elbow. "Come on, Frank. Just get some wood on it."

"Please!" adds Gord, who's sitting on the bench next to me.

Weschuk delivers Frank another fastball. He swings and misses.

Strike three. Three out. No runs. Three men left on base. Coach stamps the dirt at his feet, then kicks at a clump of grass. At the end of two, it's still Giants 3, Red Sox 1.

It's hard being on the bench in a game like this. You wish you could go out there and help. That you could try to make something happen for the team. I'm frustrated right now. I want to help.

Kelly sits by me whenever she's not up to bat or on deck. She tries to make me feel better about not playing. I tell her

I'm OK. We case Weschuk until I think we've got his pitching totally figured out.

In the top of the fifth Jeff starts throwing mostly curve balls. The Giants haven't got a chance. These are the best curve balls I've seen Jeff throw. The wickedest. They curve their way right around the Giants bats. And Frank, crouching down a little farther back from the plate than usual, is there to catch them. Not a single one slips by him. But the score's still 3 to 1.

Our guys run back to the bench. They're tired now, drinking a lot of water. Their faces are droopy. We try everything, but nothing's happening. Mrs. Minuk calls out the next three batters. Merv, Glen and Frank. Coach calls us all together.

"We have to do something," Coach shouts. "We're stuck in neutral and we're just not moving."

"Weschuk's just too hot tonight," Gord says.

"His stuff's amazing," Mitch adds.

Jeff is sitting on the bench away from everybody, splashing water from the thermos over his face. His uniform's drenched around the neck, and his long hair is matted close to his head.

"Coach, we've got to bring Poulos into the game," he says.

I'm stunned. It takes a while for the words to sink in. When they do, I don't know what to make of them. I'm totally lost.

"He's a good batter." Jeff continues. "We need him right now if we want to win this game."

I can't believe what Jeff has just said. And why? All of a sudden I feel like I'm in a dream and for some reason I'm not certain yet whether it's a good or bad one. At least I know for sure now that Jeff has noticed that I'm pretty good up at the plate. I'm sure glad Kelly convinced me to stick with the team.

Coach glances over at the diamond. Weschuk is still warming up.

"Maybe you're right," Coach says.

None of the other guys say anything.

Then Frank speaks. "Put him in for me," he says. "I'm hitting lousy."

I look at Frank then. He's not mad. He just looks like he wants to win this game.

"But what about catching?" Gord asks. "Jeff is still throwing his curve."

"I'm going to do it anyhow," Coach says. "We need some hits. Tom, you're in for Frank. You're batting after Glen. You're ready, aren't you?"

My throat's dry. Like gravel. I have to struggle to say, "Yeah."

The guys pat me on the back. Kelly brings me the bat I use and hands it to me. "Start warming up, Tom. We need you. I know you can do it."

Merv moves into the batter's box. Glen grabs a bat and starts swinging in the on deck circle. The crowd goes nuts. The Giants fans are cheering Weschuk on, our fans are cheering Merv on. But I can't hear a thing. There's a buzz in my head, but it has nothing to do with the fans. I've moved outside the dugout with my bat and swing it now. Back and forth, back and forth, cutting as even a swing as possible. I'm going to play in this game after all.

# 18

# Curve Ball!

It's a good thing I'm used to batting lead-off. I'm not afraid to bat cold, to just step up to the plate and do my job. Which is exactly what I have to do now as a pinch-hitter for Frank.

I need to somehow feel connected to the game, to bring myself closer to it. I drop down on one knee and pick up a handful of black dirt from the ground. I rub the dirt into my hands. I feel like a warrior preparing for battle. The dry dirt hardens my hands, toughens them. I grip the bat tightly around the handle.

My eyes are on Wes Weschuk up on the mound. I'm following his every move, checking out his delivery, how he throws what he throws. It's time to put to use all the preparing I've done with Kelly.

After Merv flies out to deep centrefield, Glen's up and I'm on deck. I'm using two bats at once now, swinging them around. That way when I get up to bat, the one bat will seem even lighter.

I sweep a glance over the crowd in the stands and see Uncle Nick. My eyes don't meet his. It's better that way. I just want to concentrate on getting a hit. But it's nice knowing he's up there.

And seeing him reminds me I could use a dried fig right about now. I guess I'm like those superstitious ballplayers you always hear about, but it just seems whenever I munch on a dried fig, I play my best. It's weird, but it works.

As Weschuk delivers his pitch, Glen springs into a bunting stance. His bat meets the ball with the part just opposite the label. The ball rolls into the grass towards the pitcher. Glen takes off for first. Weschuk scrambles for the ball. His fingers get lost in the grass. Glen sprints into first base. Weschuk's throw is two steps too late. It's my turn now.

I walk up to the plate. The noise from the crowd is just a drone in my ears, the way sounds'll come to you when you're underwater. I dig my running shoes into the dirt. I don't look at anyone or anything except the pitcher and the ball in his left hand. I choke up on the bat for extra control. I take three practice swings, cutting as evenly across the strike zone as possible. I press my bat up over my shoulder and lean back to wait for the pitch.

My eyes are glued on Weschuk. I see him kick his right leg out, and bring his left arm back. I see the number 7 on the chest of his uniform and how it crinkles to form a 1 when he brings his left arm up and around. I see his left hand releasing the ball. I see the ball hurtling towards me.

Right away I know it's a fastball, headed for the outside corner of the strike zone. My body loosens and prepares. I start my swing. I take a short step forward with my left foot as I bring the bat around. Then I push with my back foot, getting all the power I can from my arms, back and shoulders. All the time my eyes stay on the ball. The bat's coming around evenly. I see the bat collide with the ball. *Thwack!* The sound shoots through me like a surge of energy. My wrists turn and I follow through with the swing, drilling the ball between the second and first basemen.

The crowd's roar rings in my ears. I race for first and see Glen bounding for second. I'm almost out of breath and I'm not even at first yet. The rightfielder moves in to pick up the ball on its first hop. Glen's already on his way to third. The fielder throws the ball to second. I stay on first. Glen's safe on third.

Coach claps his hands from over behind third. "Great hit! Just what we needed," he shouts.

"Way to go, Tom," I hear Kelly calling out from the dugout.

I catch my breath. I've placed a nice hit and put a man in scoring position. I've done my job. So far.

At the plate Kelly takes her practice swings. She sneaks a playful look at me on first, like she's saying, *Isn't this fun!* Seeing her cool even in a pressure situation like this loosens me up.

Weschuk starts his windup. Kelly readies herself. The pitch is inside. Kelly backs off a few centimetres, then takes a swipe at the ball, knocking it towards the shortstop. I take off for second, but the throw beats me by a whole metre. The second baseman tries to turn the double play, but Kelly's too fast. She's safe on first. Meanwhile, Glen's made it home to score a run.

I hurry back to the bench, flying on air. I'm out, but I feel like I just hit a grand-slam homer. The guys jump all over me.

"I knew you'd come through for us, Tom," Frank says. "That was a nice hit."

"Good hit, " Jeff says. "Maybe we can still win."

I can't figure Jeff out. I suppose I'm just relieved now that he's finally realized we're both on the same team.

We end the fifth inning with the score West Side Giants 3, Windsor Park Red Sox 2. I pull on the catcher's equipment. I have to make several adjustments because Frank's so much bigger than I am, and he's let out all the straps. I panic and start to think maybe I won't be able to adjust the equipment so that I feel comfortable in it. I know I have to cool down, not think like that.

Then Coach calls me over to where he's talking with Jeff. I finish up with my equipment as best I can and hustle over. My mask's wedged under my right shoulder. My shin pads slap against my knees.

"Listen, guys, and listen close. We have to hold the Giants now. Have to. Jeff is going to be mixing his pitches. Curve balls will be part of that mix. Tom, you have to catch them. I don't know what else I can say."

"Maybe I can give Tom some sort of signal when I'm going to be throwing a curve," Jeff suggests.

"Good idea," Coach says. "Tug on your cap two times for a curve. Two times. OK, Jeff?"

I'm thinking, wow, this is sure a new Jeff I'm seeing today. I guess he really wants to win. And I can understand that. Because so do I.

"Got it, Coach."

"Got it, Tom?"

"Got it."

"Good luck, guys."

Jeff moves over to the mound. Frank is there to catch his warmup pitches. I get comfortable in my equipment and take a few deep breaths. The guys are leaving me alone, but I can tell they're looking at me, wondering if I can pull this off.

Finally, I move onto the diamond and take my place behind the plate. Frank wishes me luck. I pull on my mask and crouch down. Jeff throws me a few practice pitches.

"Play ball!"

The first batter's Kotyluk, the speedster. Jeff teases him with two outside pitches, but I lean out to nab them. I'm determined not to let anything by me. It's only one inning. I can hold on.

The batter connects on the third pitch. The ball takes a weird jump right in front of Gord at short. It must hit a pebble or something and goes flying straight up, like water out of a whale's snout. It falls in that dead area between the infield and outfield. Nobody's there to nab it. The batter's safe on third.

Jeff delivers a change-up to the next batter, Johnson. He steps into the pitch and wallops the ball high. But foul.

Jeff shakes his head. That was a close call. He smacks the side of his glove with his right hand. I bounce on the balls of my feet ready for the next pitch. Jeff tugs at the bill of his cap. Once. Then twice.

A jolt runs through my body. I scrunch back a few centimetres, carefully, so nobody notices. I don't want the Giants to catch on to what I'm doing. I smack my mitt three times. I wait. I stare at Jeff the way I would at the opposing pitcher if I were up at bat. The ball comes, streaking straight for the plate. The batter swings and misses. I'm far enough back that I see the ball curve inside. I slide my mitt to my left. The ball sails right into it. I can feel the ball sting my palm.

I've just caught my first curve ball.

Ever.

I whip that ball back to Jeff, smiling. He catches it and tugs at his cap again. Twice. I set myself up same as last time, a little back to be able to wait on that curve. The ball comes. Johnson swings. He misses. The ball breaks high and outside. I spring up to catch it.

Strike three is safe and sound in my catcher's mitt.

I wing the ball over to Kelly, and she sends it around the infield. Our guys are cheering, howling, yelling. Coach is almost dancing he's so happy. I can hear Uncle Nick's piercing whistle coming from behind me in the stands.

Stemkowski blasts Jeff's next pitch. It sails high into the sky. Miles runs after it like a madman. There's a chance he can catch it. He throws up his left arm and opens his glove up wide. The ball pounds right into it. Batter out! But Kotyluk tags up on third base and races home. Miles makes the throw, but it's not even close.

When Jeff strikes out the next batter to end the top of the sixth inning, the score's Giants 4, Red Sox 2.

Weschuk's back on the mound. The Giants coach would have been crazy to pull him now. Miles is at the plate. He's got Weschuk's number, knows how to rile him. He crowds the plate. Weschuk's pitches are missing their target. Miles walks on five pitches.

With one man on now and none out, our hopes are really alive. The tying run is at the plate, winning on deck. We're all standing on the bench in the dugout, following the action like we're out there at bat ourselves. But all Mitch can manage is a sacrifice bunt, advancing Miles to second. Then Merv pops up for the second out. All of a sudden the game's just about over. You can see it in the faces of the Giants players, and in their bodies. They can taste the victory it's so close now. They're hopping around at their bases like they're just waiting for the signal to throw their gloves high into the air and start celebrating.

I'm on deck, and Glen's up. He's cool at the plate and waits Weschuk out. All the way to four balls and a free walk to first base.

I step up to the plate. Miles and Glen are on base. There are two out. I'm the winning run. If I get can get home now, we win the twelve-year-old Little League championship game. If I get out, the Red Sox lose. We're history. I don't think I've ever been so nervous before in my life. I also don't think I'd rather be anyplace else right now but here in the batter's box.

"Come on, Tom," Kelly shouts from the on deck circle. "Keep us alive."

I concentrate. I follow Weschuk as he winds up. He uncorks a fastball. I bring my bat around to meet it. Ball hits wood. The ball sails far into right field. I've gotten a lot of power behind it. This could be a homer. I pray the ball stays fair. I take off for first. The ball veers foul. I shrug and hustle back to the plate.

But after connecting solidly like that, I'm thinking maybe I can end this game right now with a homer. Wouldn't that be great! Everybody would forget I was ever the loser who couldn't catch curve balls. I bear down at the plate and hope for another fastball. In my mind I see myself blasting the ball high over the right field fence. I'll be the hero. The Red Sox'll throw me up onto their shoulders and carry me around the ballpark. Tom Poulos, Home Run Hero.

The pitch comes. I swing. I put everything I have into it. Too much. The bat slips from my hands and goes flying into the backstop. My body twists into a pretzel. Strike two.

I step out of the batter's box. I shake my head. Who did I think I was? I'm no home run hitter. I've never in my life hit a home run in league ball. I've been getting hits on the Red Sox by concentrating on laying wood on the ball, not by dreaming about home runs.

Again I keep my eyes fixed on Weschuk. I follow his wrist as it snaps, releasing the ball. The ball shoots towards me. It's a fastball, just outside, not as far as last time. It's too close to pass up. I don't want to end this game by being called out on strikes. I step into the ball. My bat flattens it and sends it arcing over the shortstop's head. It bloops into the near outfield. Miles races home. Glen reaches third. I stay put on first.

My hit's just a single, but it brings in one run, making the score Giants 4, Red Sox 3. I'm no hero, but I did my job. And I know now that's what's most important.

Kelly's at bat. It's all up to her.

Weschuk's sweating on the mound. He brings up the sleeve of his uniform and wipes his forehead. I take a good lead off first and look out into the stands and see Uncle Nick. He blasts a loud whistle when he notices me looking up at him.

The first two pitches are balls. That makes it much easier for Kelly. The Giants are tense now. I'm not sure they can taste victory anymore. The infielders are leaning over, gloves poised, shouting instructions at one another.

Weschuk pitches. It's a fastball. Kelly uncoils her bat. She connects. The ball soars into the outfield. I take off. So does Glen. The rightfielder has to backtrack to keep up with the ball. But the ball's way behind him, dropping in deep right field. He catches up to it on the first bounce and turns around to throw to the relay man. Glen's already crossed home to tie up the game and I'm about a metre from third. All the guys on the bench are shouting "Go for it!" Coach is at third base and his right arm's whirring around like the blades of a motor. He wants me to try for home, too.

I round third, trying to keep my turn tight so as not to waste even a split second. I'm halfway home when the first baseman catches the ball from right field. I keep running, my feet digging hard into the dirt, my legs pumping high. The catcher positions himself with his left leg blocking the plate. But he has to face first to catch the ball. I drop down for the slide. My left leg is bent at the knee, and I'm hooking around the far side of the plate with my right leg. The ball whips into the catcher's mitt and he turns around. My toes stretch for home plate, and his mitt pounds down towards me. I slip my toes underneath the mitt. I can feel my toes brush against the plate. The mitt clamps down hard on my foot.

"Safe!"

I have no chance to get up. In the very next second all the other Red Sox have piled up on top of me. They're screaming and shouting, "Champs! Champs! Champs!" I shout too. It's a mad scramble. Everybody's jumping on everybody. Coach is laughing out loud and clapping his hands. Parents have hurried off the stands and are joining in the celebration. Kelly, Jeff, Frank, Glen, Gord, we're all in a circle jumping up and down.

I look over at the Giants. They've straggled off the diamond and huddle around their coach. Their heads are low. They kick the dirt with their cleats. They sneak looks at us, shaking their heads.

Coach Minuk asks us to line up and shake hands with the Giants. We're too excited to form a straight line, but do the best we can. The Giants want to hurry it up and get home. They say "Good game," to us and we say "Good game," back. But for the first time I can remember in a game I've played both teams really mean it.

Then the league commissioner walks out to us. He's wearing a suit and looks out of place on the baseball diamond. Two guys are behind him with huge boxes. He shakes Coach Minuk's hand, then shakes the Giants coach's hand. The coaches line the teams up again.

Our guys are shouting, "Tro-phees! Tro-phees!"

First, the Giants walk up to the commissioner and he shakes each player's hand and hands them a trophy. They don't seem too happy. Then our guys march up. The trophies we get say "Winnipeg Twelve-Year-Old Little League Champs" on them. They're gold trophies with an old-time baseball player swinging a bat. When I get my trophy, I kiss it and hold it high in the air, just like everybody else on our team.

I walk up to Jeff to tell him how well he pitched. I think this is the first time since he tried to scare me into quitting that Jeff has had to look straight at me and he doesn't seem to know what to say or do.

"Your curve ball was wicked tonight," I say. I mean it.

"You did a good job of catching it," Jeff says. We stare at each other, and for a second I think I see his arm move a little toward me, as if he wants to shake hands, but I can't be sure. I stand there, stiffly, while Jeff kicks at some dirt with the toe of his cleat.

"Well, see you around, T.O.," he says.

"Sure," I say, and I turn to go. A moment later, I feel someone tapping my shoulder. Jeff is holding out his hand.

"Hope you make it up here next year, Tom," he says, shaking my hand.

"Thanks," I say. I guess that's as close to an apology from Jeff as I'll get.

I move away and try to spot Kelly. I find her and we high-five and trade skin. Her dad's patting her on the back, telling us both how well we played. He shakes my hand.

Mr. Minuk carries two cases of Coke out of the trunk of his car to the dugout. We each dive in for a can and shake it around wildly and then rip open the cap ring and let the Coke gush out all over the place. The Coke pours over us, into our hair, everywhere. But everybody's laughing, loving every second of it.

Then I see Uncle Nick. He's standing at the side of the dugout fence, waiting for me to get through celebrating with everybody else. He's clapping his hands wildly. His white teeth are showing through his smile. His moustache shines in the sunlight.

"I'm taking off now," I say to Kelly.

"Don't forget the windup party next Thursday," she says.

I want to see Kelly before then. "Why don't you come over to the Olympic Diner sometime this week? I'll be helping Uncle Nick out for lunches."

"Sounds great," Kelly says, and smiles.

"See you."

"See you."

Feeling great, I run over to Uncle Nick and he reaches his big arms around me.

"That was a beautiful game of baseball you played today," he says.

"Thanks," I say, and I think I'm most happy right now because Uncle Nick was here to see it all.

# 19

# Until Next Year

We drive back to the Olympic Diner in time for the supper rush.

All the way there Uncle Nick excitedly replays my hits and catches. His hands have a tough time staying on the steering wheel, he gets so caught up in his descriptions. He's become a real baseball fan. I hold the championship trophy close, admiring it. I can't wait to show it to the guys on the Badgers.

The Olympic Diner parking lot is about half full. I would like to see every space taken, but Uncle Nick seems satisfied. He just smiles. "Business is picking up," he says.

Inside, Uncle Nick pushes his way through the little swing door to the kitchen. As soon as Vera sees us, she asks about the game. "How'd it go, kiddo?"

"Great!" I can't hide the fact I'm thrilled. "It was the greatest game I've ever played in."

"They won, by the way," Uncle Nick adds. "Five to four."

"Yahoo!" Vera lets out a cheerleader's yell. She kisses me on the forehead.

"Want something to eat, Tommy?" Uncle Nick asks. Vera is helping him put on his apron.

"No thanks. I think I'm just going to relax a little. I'll come back up front in a while."

"Any way you want it, winner. We'll be here."

I walk to my room in the back. I'm not too tired because I only played one-and-a-half innings, but I want to lie down and let the championship sink in.

I set my Ernie Whitt catcher's mitt on the bed and lay my head down on it. I close my eyes. The thrill of the game sweeps over me like a wave when you lie down on the sand at the edge of the beach.

After a while — I don't know how long — I jump up off the bed. I feel energized, like a battery that's just been re-charged. I grab the phone at the side of Uncle Nick's bed. I dial the operator and ask for a collect call to Toronto.

"Whom shall I say is calling?"

"Tom."

One, two, three rings.

I can just barely hear my Mom's voice over the line. "Hello?" I think I've woken her up from her evening nap.

"Collect call from Tom in Winnipeg, Manitoba. Do you accept the charges?"

"Of course." The operator hangs up. "Tom?" The connection is clearer now.

"Hi, Mom," I can't wait to tell her the news. "Guess what?"

Mom's in a fog. "Is everything OK, dear?"

"You bet! I just got back from the baseball diamond. The Windsor Park Red Sox are the new twelve-year-old Little League champs of Winnipeg. I scored the winning run!"

"Oh, Tom, that's wonderful. So, you're having fun now?"

"I love it."

We chat for a few minutes longer. Finally, Mom says, "I really miss you."

"I miss you, too, Mom."

"Say hi to your Uncle Nick."

"Sure will," I say. "Bye."

I decide to return to the front. I don't know why, but I take my new trophy and catcher's mitt with me. I guess maybe I want a reminder with me of what happened today at the ballpark.

Uncle Nick and Vera are sitting down having coffee with some customers. The rush is pretty much over, but I still see quite a few people in the diner munching on Olympic Diner Platters. There's a great smell of barbecued hamburger meat and fried onions in the air. It makes me hungry.

Uncle Nick rises from the table as soon as he sees me. "I can tell you're hungry now. What can I make for you?"

"A big fat juicy Olympic Diner Burger," I say.

"Coming right up," he says.

Uncle Nick tosses the hamburger patty on the barbecue. I move next to him and dress the bun the way I like it. I slap on some mustard and relish and heap on chili sauce.

When the patty's ready on one side, Uncle Nick flips it over with his spatula. I throw a piece of cheese on the cooked side. It melts there. Uncle Nick takes some fried onions off the grill and places them on my bun. When the burger's all done, I cut it carefully in half. Don't ask me why, but a burger always tastes better when it's cut in half.

I sit down with Uncle Nick and chomp into the Olympic Diner Burger. I love the taste. I know I'm going to miss it when I have to leave for Toronto.

"Vera baked a special dessert for you," Uncle Nick announces when I've finished the burger.

I wipe some chili from the side of my mouth with a paper napkin. "I'm ready for it," I say.

Vera pokes her head into the refrigerator and comes out with a big round chocolate cake, chocolate icing splattered all over it like she applied it with a paint brush. The cake's underneath one of those clear plastic covers. She brings the cake to where Uncle Nick and I are sitting. Then she pulls off the plastic top.

*Baseball Champ* is written in white icing on the top of the cake.

"Thanks, Vera," I say. "But what if we hadn't won today?"

"You'd still be a baseball champ," Vera says.

"Thanks."

"Where are the candles?" Uncle Nick asks.

"Candles? It's not his birthday, Nick," Vera says.

"So what? Candles are always fun on a cake."

Uncle Nick goes searching through some drawers for candles. He comes back with a package. "Here," he says. "One, two, three, four, five. For five runs today."

Five blue candles poke out of the cake. We all laugh. Uncle Nick lights the candles.

"Go on, blow them out," Uncle Nick and Vera say.

I bend over, take a deep breath and let loose. Uncle Nick is right, cake is more fun with candles.

When we finish our pieces of cake, I lean back from the table. I feel like I do after Mom's Christmas dinner. Great.

"Uncle Nick, I've sure had a lot of fun here this summer," I say.

"Oh, we still have three weeks. There's still more fun to have," he says. "Thanks to you the Olympic Diner is busy again. There'll be lots for us to do together in here. And it's fun work, you'll see. Look at me. I love it."

"I like working at the Olympic Diner, too," I say. It's true. This place is always interesting. And when it's busy and I help Uncle Nick serve all the customers, I feel useful.

I grab my trophy then and just gaze at it. As much as I'd like to show it off to my friends at home I decide there's something else I'd like to do with it even more.

"Uncle Nick," I say. "I want to give you this trophy."

"But that's your trophy," Uncle Nick says. "You earned it."

"I know. But I wouldn't have won it without your help. Without practising with you."

"Really?"

"Really."

I hand the trophy to Uncle Nick. He handles it carefully, like it's some Ancient Greek statue or something and might break.

"Thank you, Tommy," he says. "This is a beautiful trophy. I'm going to put it right here, on top of the cash register. Next to the menu board. So everybody can see it."

"It looks good there," Vera says.

"Don't think the rest of the summer is going to be all work," Uncle Nick says. "We're going to practise as well. As much as we can."

"Practise?"

"For next year's baseball season, of course. You're coming back, aren't you?"

"I sure hope so," I say.

"How about starting right now? You're not too tired are you?"

"No way," I say. If anything, I'm all keyed up for some ball right now. It's like when I watch baseball on TV. Right afterwards I want to go outside and play. If anything, winning the championship today has just made me hungry for more baseball.

"Vera, would you turn on the sign?" Uncle Nick says. "We're going out to practice."

So we walk out into the Olympic Diner parking lot then, Uncle Nick and I, with the day just falling away and the dark slowly filling the sky. I have my Ernie Whitt catcher's mitt with me, worked in now from the games I've played with the Red Sox. Uncle Nick is holding his baseball, twirling it in his palm. In his own funny way, he looks a lot like a ballplayer to me now.

We start by playing some catch. We slowly open up the space between us so we're throwing long and hard. The only sounds in the evening air are the slap of the ball against Uncle Nick's bare palm and the slap of the ball against my mitt. The two sounds are alike but different, the leather deeper, the skin sharper.

We toss the ball like that a while back and forth beneath the lights. Then Uncle Nick asks me to crouch down in front of our home plate — a garbage can cover — and he starts pitching me some fastballs, and I catch them and lob them back to him.

"Let me try something," Uncle Nick says then.

He winds up again, only slower this time, with more concentration, and when his hand releases the ball it twists, his finger pointing out at the end of the pitch.

The ball sails straight into my mitt. "Did it curve?"

I shake my head no.

Once more Uncle Nick rolls his body into a windup, the belt buckle underneath his belly catching the reflection of the gold letters from the Olympic Diner sign, and he tries another curve pitch.

But it doesn't curve.

"That one curved just a bit, didn't it?"

"No, Uncle Nick, I don't think it did."

Uncle Nick shakes his head and rubs his hands together. Then he lifts his hands out in front of his face. "Throw it back here," he says. "Let me have one more try."

I lob the ball back to Uncle Nick, and he pulls it out of the air. He starts the windup again he learned from those books on baseball. I sneak a peek at the tiny flame in the neon sign flickering brightly, and then Uncle Nick releases the ball, and right there under the gold and orange lights of the sign we both can see clearly, no question about it, that the ball all of a sudden changes direction, curving up and away from home plate at the last second.

I can't believe my eyes. Uncle Nick has just thrown a perfect curve ball. A lot of batters would be fooled by it. A lot of batcatchers would have trouble catching it.

Uncle Nick laughs out loud in the quiet night. I stretch out my arm and trap the ball in my mitt.